"Ammonia and chlorine," Red Malice said on the monitor. "Soon you will be overwhelmed by the deadly fumes of the gas."

I charged for the door, but there was no knob or handle. It was just a thick slab of steel sealing me inside. I covered my nose and mouth with my shirt. I had less than a minute to get out of the room.

"Perhaps you've noticed the window," Red Malice said teasingly. "I doubt you'll be able to escape, but by all means, try."

The window near the ceiling was just under a foot tall and about eighteen inches wide, too small for a grown-up to squeeze through, but if I exhaled all the air in my lungs, I might be able to do it.

There was a sink below the window. I leapt onto it while trying to hold my breath. I could barely reach the windowsill. As I hung against the wall, a startling realization came to me.

I was going to die if I couldn't do a chin-up.

THE AMAZING ADVENTURES OF NATE BANKS

READ THEM ALL!

RED ALERT

by
JAKE BELL

cover and comic art by
CHRIS GIARRUSSO

SCHOLASTIC INC.

New York Toronto London Auckland

Sydney Mexico City New Delhi Hong Kong

*Dedicated to the memories of
Robert Kanigher, Bob Haney,
and Otto Binder*

ISBN 978-0-545-15671-4

Text copyright © 2010 by Jake Bell
Illustrations copyright © 2010 by Scholastic Inc.
All rights reserved. Published by Scholastic Inc.
SCHOLASTIC, APPLE PAPERBACKS, THE AMAZING
ADVENTURES OF NATE BANKS, and associated logos are
trademarks and/or registered trademarks of Scholastic Inc.

12 11 10 9 8 7 6 5 4 3 2 1   10 11 12 13 14 15/0

Printed in the U.S.A.   40
First printing, October 2010

Contents

Contents

Those Jalapeños Are Spicy, President McKinley

I guess you could say it was a typical Wednesday afternoon. After a grueling day of sixth grade, I was working on a history report that was due in sixteen hours.

I knew that William McKinley had been the twenty-fifth president of the United States and the last Civil War veteran to hold the office, and that Mount McKinley in Alaska was named in his honor.

And now I also knew that he smelled *terrible*.

His corpse sat across from me at the dining room table of my friend Captain Zombie.

President McKinley leaned forward and examined the plate on the table between us. "What did you call these?" he asked in a booming voice. "Nickels?"

"Nachos," I repeated for the third time.

"Wonderful things," President McKinley said. He

scooped up a cheese-coated chip with fingers of bone held loosely together with rotting tendons. Then he swiped the chip around the plate to make sure he got a sampling of salsa, sour cream, and olive. "We certainly didn't have this delicacy in my day!"

He dropped the chip into his mouth, which hinged open in an unnatural way, making him look like a snake preparing to swallow a mouse. As he chewed, bits of the nacho fell through a hole beneath his chin, where his flesh had rotted away. Shards of chips and dribbles of sour cream dropped onto his moth-eaten suit.

I shot a frustrated glance at Captain Zombie, who smiled and gave me two thumbs-up for encouragement. Behind him, my best friends, Teddy and Fiona, watched in disgust.

I pressed on with the interview, moving to the next question in my notebook. "How did it feel to add a new state to the country?"

"A new state?" he asked, looking puzzled. He reached for the plate of nachos again.

"Hawaii."

"What's that?" he asked. "Hawai'i was granted statehood?" He leaned back in his chair and slapped his knee happily. "I wish William Jennings Bryan and

Henry Adams could hear that. What say you about my imperialist outlook now, Adams?"

I sighed. My interview wasn't going very well. Captain Zombie had tried to warn me when I'd first proposed it. Apparently, it's hard to keep the living dead on topic. They're so interested in catching up on what they've missed that they wind up doing more asking than answering. It's not the best situation when you're trying to conduct an interview.

Still, I desperately needed to pull up my history grade before the end of the semester. When my teacher, Ms. Matthews, had assigned us reports on former presidents and I had drawn McKinley's name, I had figured that Captain Zombie was the key to my success. I knew I wasn't going to get away with rewording the article about William McKinley from Wikipedia. Ms. Matthews was way too smart for that. To impress her, I would need Captain Zombie's ability to speak to the dead.

I begged him for a week. Then I finally got him to agree, after I beat him at a game of Pictionary with a little help from Teddy. Somehow, I'd assumed that once I walked down the steps into Captain Zombie's secret mausoleum headquarters, the former president of the United States would just open up and practically write the paper for me, but that wasn't proving to be the case. Teddy and Fiona had been smart to do their reports the old-fashioned way.

McKinley shoveled another nacho into his mouth between happy chuckles. "Say there, lad, what did you call these green things?"

"Jalapeños," I replied. "Be careful—they're spicy."

"Tell me more," he insisted as he topped his next chip with a small slice of jalapeño. "What about the Philippines? Has that become a state as well?"

"No."

"Cuba?"

"No."

"Don't tell me they've both fallen back to the Spaniards."

"No, they're both their own countries now."

"Whooo!" the president hollered as he fanned his mouth with a decrepit hand.

"I told you they were spicy," I reminded him.

Captain Zombie stepped forward with a fresh glass of soda for President McKinley, who gulped it down.

But the president wasn't paying attention to me. Instead, he was studying his drink. He dunked his fingers into the glass and fished out an ice cube. Then he held it up to the milky orbs that were the remains of his eyes.

"Your ice," he said in awe, "it's nearly a perfect rectangle."

"Yes, sir," Captain Zombie answered, giving me a reassuring smile. "We call them ice cubes."

"Will wonders never cease?" the president mused.

"Nate, perhaps this is a bit much for the president to take in all at once," Captain Zombie suggested. He turned to McKinley. "Sir, perhaps we should take a break. Would you like to play a parlor game of sorts? We call it Pictionary. You can have Teddy on your—"

"I'm not so sure that's a good idea," I interjected. After McKinley's reaction to the ice cube, who knew what would happen if he had to draw a calculator or a cell phone? "Maybe we should just call it a night."

President McKinley nodded. Then he leaned in close.

"Son, do you know what the last thing I ate was?" he asked softly.

"Er, no," I replied. Captain Zombie had warned me about this, too. Freshly raised corpses tended to be pretty hungry. That was why Captain Zombie had put out some snacks for the former president.

"A piece of toast with a cup of coffee," McKinley said

sadly. "Bitter, weak coffee. I thought nothing of it at the time. I was recovering in a hospital bed. The doctors said I was healthy enough to have a little something to eat, and that's what they brought me. Had I known it would be my last meal, I would have ordered a steak as thick as a dictionary."

"You mentioned William Jennings Bryan before. Let me just ask—"

"Smothered in sautéed mushrooms and onions."

"You campaigned against Bryan twice—"

"Oh, and a twice-baked potato," he whispered.

"What did you think of Bryan as an opponent?"

"Bryan was a clown," he grumbled, snapping out of his food reverie.

And with that, he scooped another pile of cheese, ground beef, salsa, and jalapeños onto a chip and tossed it into his mouth.

"I hate to bring up the, er, assassination," I said hesitantly. I was nervous about asking him about his death, but I knew I had to. It was an important part of my report.

"A hospital bed is a terrible place to die," he replied with a sigh.

"Huh?" I asked as I flipped back through the notes I'd taken. "I thought you were shot at the World's Fair."

"Yes, but I didn't die there," McKinley answered. "I survived another nine days, fading in and out. The doctors didn't realize my wounds were infected. They told me I would make a full recovery, but they didn't know gangrene had already poisoned my blood. A man doesn't last long under those circumstances."

"Do you know why that guy wanted to kill you?" I asked. "Why didn't he like you as president?"

"I don't think he cared what kind of president I was. I think he felt powerless and wanted to lash out at the most powerful man in the country." He frowned and his voice grew raspy. "Lying in that hospital bed, I found I could relate. In the pull of a trigger, I'd gone from a man who commanded armies and navies around the globe to a man who couldn't dress himself or eat solid food."

"I don't get it," I said. "How did that help you relate to the guy who shot you?"

"Because when I lay there in that bed, I knew death was coming for me. I would have given anything to feel as though I was in control of my own destiny. It wasn't that I was going to die that bothered me—it was that I had no say in how or when or why."

I scribbled some notes as he spoke.

"Mark my words, lad," he declared loudly, tapping my notebook and leaving a dusty mark. "Any man who finds himself powerless is capable of anything if he thinks it will return to him a sense of power. And when we've lost power, our beliefs are all we have left, so we cling to them, even when they cease to matter. In fact, that's when we cling hardest. Our regrets and our desires take on much greater importance."

The intensity in what remained of his milky eyes seemed to burn through me. I wrote his words down but was relieved when Captain Zombie stepped in again.

"That's probably a good stopping point," he said. "What do you say, Nate? Can I take President McKinley back now?"

The president grabbed fistfuls of nachos with both hands and stuffed them into his pockets. "Thank you, Mr. President," I said, standing. "I'm sure this will help with my history report."

"Glad to help, my boy."

I gathered my papers and slipped them into my

backpack. "You mind if we get home?" I asked Captain Zombie. "These reports are due tomorrow."

"Go ahead," he said with a flash of his yellowed teeth. "I'll make sure he gets back where he belongs."

Outside the mausoleum door Teddy, Fiona, and I hopped on our bicycles. "So?" I asked both my friends.

"I'm kind of glad I didn't ask him to do Chester Arthur for me now," Teddy admitted. "I can just imagine him plowing through a cheeseburger while I try to ask him about civil service reform."

"Same here," Fiona agreed. "I was picturing Franklin Pierce and a plate of buffalo wings the whole time."

"Well, I wrote down everything he said," I replied as I pushed off. "I might be able to find something useful in my notes."

We pedaled through the cemetery gates and headed for home.

It's Not a Bookshelf

A few days later, for the first time I could remember, it was the day before winter break and my end-of-the-semester grades weren't an issue, at least not with my parents. They had lowered their expectations long before. Sure, they still had dreams that I'd become a straight-A student like my sister, Denise, but given my past track record, they'd celebrate anything higher than a C.

I realized that my report card just might be allowed to hang on the fridge next to Denise's rather than tucked slightly behind it. My parents seemed to think I didn't notice the way they usually strategically covered my grades with her report card, just in case company dropped in.

I knew I had an A in science, because our substitute teacher, Mrs. Sutcliffe, was a home ec teacher who knew nothing about science. She told us she'd give everyone As as long as we promised to watch the big meteor shower over winter break. Mr. Dawson had given my book report on *The Old Man and the Sea* an A-minus, which gave me a solid B in English. And Mrs. Clemente let me know that despite getting a 79 percent on the algebra final, I'd still pulled off a B in math as well. Coach Howard hadn't taken any pity on me when I'd slipped during the shuttle run, so I wound up with a C in gym. But I wasn't too worried. It wasn't like I was going to die if I couldn't do a chin-up. And Mr. Bench let me off with a B in woodshop even though the varnish on the step stool I'd built had pooled into sticky brown globs.

As long as I managed a B average, I figured I'd be fine. After all, that was what Doctor Nocturne had told me I needed to maintain my position as Ultraviolet's advisor. That was after Phantom Ranger asked Doctor Nocturne to help train me. You would think it would have been Ultraviolet's call, but when Doctor Nocturne and Phantom Ranger told you how things were going to be, the rest of the superhero community kind of went right along.

History class was the only remaining question mark, and I was hovering right around a 78 percent. Ironically, my history teacher, Ms. Matthews, just happened to *be*

Ultraviolet. To remain Ultraviolet's advisor, I had to ace Ms. Matthews's president report.

Even though we'd turned in our reports only the day before, Ms. Matthews had promised she'd have them graded by the end of Friday. For most teachers, that would have been impossible. But Ms. Matthews was different. When a class ended, she could fly downtown, save a dozen people trapped in a fire, nab a guy swiping chrome rims off a Mercedes, find a lost puppy, and get back before the bell rang for the next period. So I doubted that reading through a couple dozen three-page papers was going to offer her much of a challenge.

When the final bell of the day rang, most of the school hurried for the exits. I headed toward the social studies wing to hear the verdict. There was no way I could wait a week to find out. How could I enjoy Christmas knowing that somewhere between the Kanigher Falls Public School District and the post office there was a slip of paper that would determine my entire future?

"Something's wrong with your bookshelf," Teddy observed as I sped out of the woodshop.

"It's a step stool," I said, correcting him.

He raised an eyebrow while eyeing the item in my

hands. "I'm not saying it looks like a bookshelf, but it looks more like a bookshelf than a stool."

We waited a moment for Fiona to join us. She was carrying her own woodshop project.

"That doesn't look like a step stool, either," Teddy noted. "That looks more like a spice rack."

"It *is* a spice rack," she said, rolling her eyes. "I finished my step stool two weeks ago. This was an extra-credit project I built to give my mom for Christmas."

"Did your stool look like this?" he asked, grabbing mine and holding it up for her to see.

"No," I interrupted, grabbing back my project. "She got an A-plus, and hers had a perfectly even mahogany stain. It also didn't give the teacher a splinter when he examined it. Are you happy now?"

Teddy suddenly released my step stool and began examining his fingers for slivers.

I hustled down the hallway toward Ms. Matthews's classroom, knowing we had a bus to catch back to our side of town. Our school, Ditko Middle School, had been destroyed in a battle between Ultraviolet and Dr. Malcontent, who had been our science teacher at the time. Until the school could be rebuilt, all the Ditko students were being bused across town to and from Eisner Middle

School, and that meant we had to be on board by 3:35 in the afternoon or risk being left behind.

"Where are you going?" Teddy asked. He and Fiona followed me, fighting their way through the pack of students heading for the exit.

"I have to talk to Ms. Matthews."

"But we have to get to the bus."

"We're not going to miss the bus," I assured them. I was certain the bus driver, Mr. Mazzilli, wouldn't leave without us. I'd saved his life a few months earlier, and I figured the least he could do was hold the bus for a few minutes. "I need to check on my McKinley report."

I could see that both were reluctant to chance it, but their expressions changed quickly. "Teddy!" called out Allison Heaton. At the tall, blond seventh grader's voice, Teddy swooned. And Fiona looked like someone had hit her in the back of the head with my step stool.

"Hey, Allison," Teddy singsonged dreamily.

"Where are you guys going?" Allison asked.

"We have to check our grades with Ms. Matthews," Fiona insisted, dragging Teddy and me away.

"Oh, then I'll come with you," Allison said. Fiona rolled her eyes at me and pretended to gag herself.

I entered Ms. Matthews's room to find her filling a

box with her teaching supplies, packing up in preparation to move into the new Ditko come January. She smiled when she saw me, but screwed up her face into a scowl and got back into character when she saw the others tagging along. Teddy and Fiona both knew she was Ultraviolet. In fact, the three of us and my sister were the only ones in town who had a clue. Ms. Matthews couldn't risk dropping the act in front of Allison.

"Oh, Nate," she said sharply. "I expected that with the semester at a close, you'd be one of the first ones out the door." She nodded to my friends. "Did you want your grades, too?"

"That's okay," Teddy replied. "We're just here to see if Nate gets to keep being a superh—" Fiona elbowed him sharply in the ribs.

Ms. Matthews glared at Teddy. Finally, she returned her attention to me. "Well, Nate, I read"—she picked up the paper and read the title—"'Shot Down in a Blaze of Glory: An Essay on William McKinley.'"

I braced myself.

"I'm very impressed by your analysis of American expansionism in the late nineteenth and early twentieth centuries. You showed a lot of insight into McKinley's views on the subject. There are biographies of McKinley that aren't this perceptive."

So far, so good.

"I had to take off some points for spelling and punctuation, though. And nachos weren't invented until the 1940s, so I had to take off a point for this paragraph you included about how much the president loved them."

"Not to rush you, but we're going to miss the bus," Fiona chimed in.

Ms. Matthews showed me the paper. At the top, she had written *A: Very Good Work, Nate* in red ink.

"That means I finished the semester with—"

"A B-plus," she told me with a grin. "And if you had been doing this kind of work all semester, you would have had an A, without a doubt."

I heaved a sigh of relief. I threw up my hand for a high five. Unfortunately, I had forgotten about Ms. Matthews's superstrength.

"Ow!" I shouted as I shook my stinging hand. She just smiled at me.

"Now, hurry up," she said. "You're going to miss your bus."

Choo-Choo Train Jammies

My big news didn't get the reaction I was hoping for at dinner. I should have known that an A, four Bs, and a C in gym couldn't compare to Denise's straight As. After all, Denise had been bringing home nothing but As for three years. The only reason that streak wasn't longer was that she'd gotten a B-plus in fifth-grade English because she had insisted on dotting her *i*'s with smiley faces and using hearts for periods for a semester.

So Denise's good grades were no surprise, but I thought mine were. After all, I had coasted by for the last few years pulling plenty of Cs, and suddenly I had a solid B average. I figured that was something to get worked up about. My parents didn't seem to agree, though.

While both of them offered the obligatory "Good job," my dad's focus fell sharply on the grade for gym. And my mom felt that the upturn in my grades only added credence to her long-standing theory that I hadn't been living up to my potential. She claimed I was just too lazy to get grades like Denise's.

"If you can turn things around in less than half a semester, I don't see why you shouldn't be able to get straight As by the end of the year," she said.

"Your mom's right," my dad said encouragingly. "In January you'll have a clean slate."

I wanted to tell them a B average was good enough for Ultraviolet. It was good enough for Doctor Nocturne. It was good enough for the Phantom Ranger, the world's most popular superhero. Even my mom considered herself a Phantom Ranger fan. Denise could have her straight As. I didn't see Lady Bullet or Jade Mask offering her an advisory position. But of course I couldn't say any of that.

After dinner, I got on the computer to read a few comic blogs and to see what I was in for when my friends and I picked up our weekly hauls at Funny Pages the next day. At least I could talk to them about Ultraviolet, and they understood what my B average really meant.

Later that night, I brushed my teeth and changed into some flannel pants before I hopped into bed. But

I couldn't fall asleep. Instead, I tossed around restlessly, wondering how long it would take for word to spread about my good grades among the superhero community. The harder I tried, the harder it was to fall asleep. I must have started to drift off, because my sleepy thoughts were suddenly interrupted by shouts from Doctor Nocturne.

"Nate Banks." His deep voice with its southern accent echoed in my head. "We need to talk."

A part of me recognized that I was dreaming, and Doctor Nocturne was using his telepathic powers to invade my subconscious. This wasn't the first time he'd contacted me this way, and fortunately, I knew what to expect.

Among Doctor Nocturne's mysterious powers was telepathy. He could project images and sounds into people's minds. The first time he'd done it to me, he'd interrupted one of my dreams. Afterward, I had been left wondering whether it had really happened. This time, though, it sounded like he was in the room with me.

"Come talk to me," he said firmly.

"I'm right here," I replied slowly. For some reason, I sounded like I was really far away from my body.

"No, not *here*," he answered, sounding annoyed. "I said come talk to me. I'm outside."

Slowly, I opened one eye to see the bright green numbers of my alarm clock, which read 10:45. I hadn't been asleep at all. But then why had I heard Doc—

Suddenly, there was a loud rap on the window. I got out of bed and tiptoed over cautiously. I pulled back the curtains and peered outside. A large man in a blue suit was leaning on a cane and impatiently shaking a handful of pebbles. He must have tossed one at my window to get my attention. He had an angry, no-nonsense scowl on his face, and he was pointing at the back door.

The TV was on in my parents' bedroom, and I hoped that would cover the sound of my creeping down the stairs. My jacket hung on a chair near the back door, so I put it on over my pajamas and quietly slipped out the door.

"What took you so long?" Doctor Nocturne demanded before I could latch the door behind me.

"What do you mean?" I replied defensively. "I came right down. I had to be quiet or my parents would have heard me."

"Well, I hope if Terrorantula unleashes an army of robotic spiders on downtown Kanigher Falls, he'll be polite enough not to disturb your parents."

"Terrorantula is downtown?" I shouted.

"No! Now, be quiet," he said, hushing me. "You're going to disturb your parents."

"But you said—"

He sighed heavily.

"I just meant that you need to be ready at all times. When someone calls a superhero for help, you can't dilly-dally, creeping down the stairs and—" He stopped and eyed me from head to toe suspiciously. "Are you wearing pajamas?"

"I told you I came right down. I didn't have time to change."

Doctor Nocturne rubbed his temples and bit his lower lip. "Boy, when the fate of the world hangs in the balance, you can't be rushing to save the day in choo-choo train jammies."

"There's no choo-choo—"

"And can't you get down here any faster?" Doctor Nocturne went on, leaning impatiently on his cane and staring up at my bedroom window. "Don't you have any kind of secret exit up there?"

"No," I told him. "Not many suburban houses include hidden passageways."

"We're going to have to add that to the list," he said as he scribbled something in a small notebook. He slid the notebook into his pocket and gestured toward the alley beside my house with the handle of his cane, which was carved to resemble the horse-headed knight chess piece. "Follow me."

As Doctor Nocturne walked, I could tell he was trying not to limp, though every few steps, I could see him favor his bad leg.

"What are you thinking about?" he barked. "I can hear the gears grinding in that head of yours."

"Nothing," I shot back. "Nice night, isn't it? Chilly for me, but I guess in Kurtzburg this is practically spring weather."

He looked at me skeptically while he opened the gate that led to the back alley. A large dark blue motorcycle with a sidecar was parked beside the garbage cans. Doctor Nocturne gazed up and down the alley like something was missing.

"What are you looking for?" I whispered.

"Why are you whispering?" he whispered back.

"Sorry," I said, raising my voice to a normal volume. "It just feels like we're sneaking—"

"We're supposed to be meeting someone, but it seems she's late."

As if on cue, Ultraviolet descended from the starry sky. She pulled off her purple-tinted goggles.

"Nate?" she asked. "It's eleven at night. What are you doing—are you in your pajamas?"

"Yes, but they don't have choo-choo trains on them," I said.

Ultraviolet opened her mouth as if to speak, but then she stopped herself. She turned to Doctor Nocturne, who was grabbing a helmet from the sidecar. "What did you need to discuss that was so important you pulled him out of bed this late?"

"I've been working with the contractors who are building your secret headquarters," he started. "There have been a few snags, but these guys can do a hidden lair in their sleep, so it's nothing to worry about."

"I'm sorry," Ultraviolet interrupted. "Did you say 'secret headquarters'?"

"He also said 'hidden lair,'" I said excitedly.

Doctor Nocturne pitched me the helmet. "Hop in," he said as he gestured toward the bike. "You won't miss too much beauty sleep."

A B Average Doesn't
Get You Anything

Doctor Nocturne dropped the motorcycle into gear and flew down the alley like a bullet down the barrel of a gun. I was thankful the deafening roar of the engine drowned out my screams of terror as we screeched onto Lampert Avenue. A few quick turns later, and he killed the engine in the parking lot of Ditko Middle School. Ultraviolet landed right beside us. She looked as surprised as I was.

The three of us stood amid the construction project. During Ultraviolet's battle with Dr. Malcontent, my two teachers had grappled in the sky high above the school and then crashed to Earth with enough power to drive them through the roof, floor, and foundation of the school.

"This will be the primary entrance," Doctor Nocturne explained as he gestured toward the hole they'd left.

It didn't look like a primary entrance. It didn't look like anything other than a hole in the ground. But then, I guessed if it *looked* like a secret entrance, it wouldn't be much of a secret.

Doctor Nocturne explained that the impact from Ultraviolet and Dr. Malcontent's battle had already done most of the excavating for the elevator shaft that would lead from a janitor's closet to the underground lair.

"My underground lair is going to be under the *school*?" Ultraviolet asked skeptically. "Isn't that a bit dangerous?"

"What better place for your secret headquarters than one that's right near where you spend most of your time?" Doctor Nocturne replied. "There will be more than one entrance. Ultraviolet, we can't get a tunnel to your current apartment because it's on the second floor. So it's been arranged for you to move into a first-floor condominium. The movers will be there on the twenty-eighth." He fished a set of keys from his pocket. "The address is on this tag," he pointed out.

Ultraviolet took the keys suspiciously, holding the key ring between her thumb and forefinger at arm's length.

"I'm not going to worry about a tunnel for Nate until we know whether he's going to make the cut," he continued. "Construction crews will be working through the holidays, and you should be operational by the new year."

I was so caught up in staring down the hole, imagining banks of computers and satellite monitors and crime lab equipment, that it took a second before I registered what he'd said. *Make the cut?*

"Good news," I assured him. "You said if I averaged a B, I was in. I got an A, four Bs, and a C. That's a B average. So I guess you can start building that tunnel."

"No, what I said was if you *didn't* average a B, you were finished," he answered, correcting me. "Getting a B average doesn't get you anything. It just means I'm not kicking you to the curb *yet*. You have two weeks off from school, and I'm going to spend every minute of it running you through the wringer." He leaned over until his eyes were inches from mine. "You want to be a superhero?" he asked menacingly. "I'm going to show you what it takes."

I raised my hand hesitantly. "To be clear, I don't want to be a superhero," I said. "I'm just an advisor. I read a lot of comic books; I follow the news; I tell her what I know about supervillains. My plan is to stay out of the way."

"Uh-huh," he grunted sarcastically. "Like you stayed out of the way when Dr. Malcontent attacked your school? And like you stayed out of the way when Coldsnap came to town? Ultraviolet's had two major fights with supervillains, and you've been smack in the middle of both of them. So tell me again how you don't need training?"

I turned to Ultraviolet for support but found her nodding. "He's got a point, Nate. I certainly could have used some training, and I'm more or less indestructible."

I wanted to point out that she got some awesome training thanks to me, but I could tell I wasn't going to win this argument. "I suppose I can try to meet up with you a few times in the next two weeks. Monday should work, but Wednesday is Christmas Eve, and then there's Christmas, and that leads right into the weekend, so it'll probably be the following Monday before I—"

Doctor Nocturne shook his head. "*Every* night."

"Are you kidding me?" Didn't he understand I was on break? I had TV to watch and presents to open and comic books to read and—

"Starting tomorrow," he ordered. "Until either you quit or you convince me you're ready."

I'd made plans to go to the comic-book store with Teddy and Fiona the next day, but I didn't get the impression he cared much about my social life, so I kept that to myself.

"And don't go blabbing about this to your little playmates," Doctor Nocturne warned. "They know too much already. You've told them Ultraviolet's secret identity and dragged them into a fight with Coldsnap. Why don't you just leave them out of this for a while?"

It should be noted that Teddy and Fiona knew Ultraviolet's secret identity because I'd bounced ideas off them while I was trying to figure it out myself. And they'd saved both Ultraviolet and me when Coldsnap had gotten the upper hand. But Doctor Nocturne didn't seem open to hearing all sides of the story.

Doctor Nocturne took me back home.

"Tomorrow I'll have my daughter meet you at the cemetery at five-thirty," he said.

"The Kurtzburg Cemetery?" I asked.

"Yes, the Kurtzburg Cemetery!" he barked back before taking a deep breath. "Don't be late." With that, he tore off down the alley again, leaving me to sneak back into my bedroom just before midnight. The TV was off now, so I had to be even more careful.

I'd have to make sure I met Captain Zombie in time. I didn't want to risk being late my first day. Kurtzburg was in Maryland, three time zones ahead of Kanigher Falls, which was in Arizona. Or was it two time zones? I tried to remember to look that up as my head hit the pillow.

NOTPASSWORD

"What's the password to get on the Internet?"

I opened my eyes slowly to let them adjust to the morning light streaming through the window.

"Gah!" Teddy's face was inches away from mine.

"What's the password to get on the Internet?" he repeated. "Is it 'password'?"

"No, it's not 'password.' What are you doing in here?"

"Fiona and I came by but your mom said you were asleep. We figured while we waited for you to get up and get ready, we'd read NotSoHeroic.com. On my grandma's computer, her password is 'password.'"

"Yeah, well, that's because she's old and you're lucky if she remembers your name." I sat up, stretched, and rubbed my eyes. "Why are you over so early? We're not supposed to go to Funny Pages until eleven."

"It's eleven-ten," he informed me. "Were you up late?"

I started to tell him about Doctor Nocturne's visit, but I realized that might violate the don't-tell-your-friends policy. "Nah, guess I'm just tired from school."

Teddy laughed. "Right, because you work so hard in school. So, can you tell me the password?"

"Well, it's definitely not 'password'—"

"Okay, got it."

He left the room before I could finish and I heard him jog down the stairs to the computer in the family room. I got out of bed and started to get dressed when I heard the pounding of footsteps coming back up the stairs.

"It's not working," Teddy announced.

"What's not working?"

"'Notpassword.' We punched it in, but the computer wouldn't let us on the Internet."

"I told you it's not 'password'—"

"Is it capitalized weird? Or does it have an 'at' sign in it or zeroes, like 'N-zero-T-P-@-S-S-W-zero-R-D?'"

"The password is *not* 'notpassword,'" I said, stopping him. "It's 'BulletHead55,' with a capital 'B' and 'H.'" My dad kept an action figure of his favorite football player, Demetrius "Bullethead" Johnson, number fifty-five on the

Everett Rhinos, on the corner of the desk as a reminder. "Now leave me alone so I can get dressed."

When I got downstairs, I could hear Teddy laughing at the computer. NotSoHeroic.com was a gossip site that posted rumors about superheroes along with photos of them at their worst. Teddy was giggling at a photo of Baron Shield fending off an attack by Snicker-Snack. The photo showed Baron Shield from behind, his trunks bunched up in the middle.

"Baron Shield with a wedgie," Teddy chuckled. "That's great stuff."

"That picture is, like, four years old," I told him.

"Yeah, but it's still funny."

"Anything new on there?"

"Moonrock is warning everyone about the meteor shower Monday night," Fiona said.

"The sky is falling! The sky is falling!" Teddy mocked.

"There's a video clip from an interview with the Blueblood." She clicked play on the image.

The Blueblood had been a superhero in the 1950s, and the older he got, the crazier his claims grew. About every year or so, someone would convince him to sit down for an interview and he would unleash a tirade about "the good old days."

"Because back then, it was about pride," the Blueblood yelled at the camera. "We didn't try to be in commercials or sell T-shirts; we just tried to make our towns safe. Heroes today should take lessons from the guys I used to work with. The guys today can't hold a candle to someone like Red—"

Fiona hit pause. "That interview was from British TV. They already posted a link to it on Monday."

"Anything else or are you guys ready to go?"

"Hang on," Teddy said. "You need to see the best one."

Fiona scrolled up to show a photo of Ultraviolet with her cape twisted up in a mass and clinging to her arms and legs like a second skin. Her hair frizzed out in all directions. Fiona read the picture's caption aloud. "'Ultraviolet has no trouble defeating Coldsnap, but static cling? Not so much.'"

I laughed, wondering if I should tell Doctor Nocturne to include a decent washer and dryer with any crime computers and video surveillance equipment in Ultraviolet's new hideout.

o o o

I'd been planning to spend hours at Funny Pages combing through the back issues to find copies of *Marauder* from the eighties, but two of the regulars,

Blubbs and Horse, were in the middle of an argument over who was the best starship captain on *Galactic Journey*. The topic of Captain Lindstrom versus Captain Hart was pretty standard among the sci-fi nerd set, but Blubbs and Horse took it to a new level.

Before they started throwing anything, Jeff, the store's owner, rang up our books and we took off, leaving the quest for back issues for a calmer day.

"Do you really think the journey is better than the destination?" Teddy asked as I unlocked my bike.

"What? Tell me you are not about to start talking about *Galactic Journey*," Fiona threatened.

"Huh?" Teddy grunted, pulling his face out of the latest issue of *Hurricane Squad*. "Oh, no, I was just reading this and there's a scene where the bad guy's got the good guy tied up and he complains because the fun is over."

I leaned over to look at the comic. Baron Cuda was giving one of those cliché supervillain monologues: "Oh, what a disappointment you've proven to be. I thought you'd be more of a challenge. Now that I've caught you so easily, I realize that the journey is greater than the destination."

"That's just comic-book melodrama," I told Teddy. "Of course the journey isn't—"

Suddenly, a high-pitched whistle pierced the air. We

craned our necks upward to see a streak of white dropping from the sky. It was clearly about to land in the middle of the shopping center parking lot.

Panicked shoppers scattered, but fortunately, there was something even faster in the sky. Twenty feet above the ground, a white and purple streak intercepted the falling object, bringing the whistling to an abrupt stop. Ultraviolet hovered above the parked cars, a piece of a meteorite about the size of a cantaloupe cradled in her arm.

My eyes met Ultraviolet's for a moment while she surveyed the crowd to make sure no one was hurt. Then she abruptly flew away.

Seconds later, a familiar voice called to me. "Nate."

I turned to see Ms. Matthews sitting at a table outside Bean There, Done That, the coffee shop next door to Funny Pages. "What are you—? Where did you go?"

"I was just inside getting a latte," she replied smoothly. She gestured toward my stack of comic books. "What new reading material did we pick up today?"

I walked to the waist-high fence that surrounded the outdoor café tables, and my friends followed. "Kind of a light week," I answered. "*Hurricane Squad, Man Ghost,* and *Tales of the Outrageous.*"

"Do you mind if I take a look?" she asked.

Teddy instinctively held his comics to his chest, like a mother protecting her young, and Fiona took a slight step backward, leaving only me to share my brand-new, perfect, mint-condition comics with our teacher. I handed her the comics and winced when she placed them on the table, just inches from her coffee cup.

She scanned the entire issue of *Hurricane Squad* in about thirty seconds. Then she flipped open *Man Ghost* but paused on page seven. "What's this?"

I looked at the image, a picture of Man Ghost talking to the police commissioner. "Well, you remember Man Ghost?" I asked. Months earlier, when I'd tried to read some comics—including *Man Ghost*—in class, Ms. Matthews had confiscated them and wound up reading them for advice on how to become a better superhero. "And that's Commissioner Moraga—"

"Where are they?"

"That's Man Ghost's office," Fiona chimed in. "It's on the top floor of a condemned building."

"His secret lair is just a regular office," Ms. Matthews said, more to herself than to us. "Do other comic books—" She stopped and cocked her head to the side, a move that always meant there was a job for Ultraviolet. "Oops, looks like I grabbed sugar instead of the no-calorie substitute," she said unconvincingly, holding up two white packets of sugar. "Excuse me for a moment."

She got up and hurried back into the coffee shop. My friends and I exchanged "can you believe that lame excuse?" glances while a white and purple blur streaked over the parking lot from behind the store.

"Sorry about that," Ms. Matthews said when she returned a few seconds later, two small yellow packets in her hand. Her hair was back in a tight bun, she was wearing her glasses, and there was no indication whatsoever that she'd been off saving the day for the past twelve seconds. "What I was asking was whether other comic-book characters have secret bases or headquarters."

"Pretty much all of them," Teddy said.

"And there's a variety, I assume," she continued.

I could see where she was going. "Sure," I replied. "There are a lot of different kinds of hidden lairs, and all of the details are in the comic books. I'm sure I have dozens of designs and ideas if I dig through my collection."

"Very interesting," she said as she handed back my comic books. "That sounds like it could make for fascinating reading." From her expression, I knew I'd be spending part of my vacation combing through my comic-book collection for information about secret hide-outs. "Well, I'm sure you guys don't want to spend your break talking to your teacher. I'll let you go."

"Okay," Teddy said quickly, clearly eager to get away. I waved politely and we all returned to our bikes.

"So what do you guys want to do tonight?" Fiona asked. "I found out I'm getting the complete *Nightowl* animated series on DVD for Christmas. If I'm careful with the tape, I can unwrap it, take out disc one, and we can watch it. Just not at my place."

"Sounds cool," Teddy replied, and it did sound cool. But I had other plans.

"Tonight's no good," I said. "I have to do this . . . thing. With, you know, my dad. We're, uh . . . shopping. Yeah! For my mom's Christmas present." The story seemed plausible to me.

"Well, tomorrow night, then," Fiona suggested.

"Works for me," Teddy agreed.

I just shrugged, hoping that in twenty-four hours I could come up with a better excuse than going shopping with my mom for my dad's Christmas present.

Try to Land Flat

When I exited the mausoleum, the sun was just setting, which took a minute to get used to. Moments earlier it had been a bright, sunny afternoon, but there was a two-hour time difference between Kurtzburg and Kanigher Falls. My parents were at my dad's office Christmas party and were under the impression that I was at Teddy's. So they wouldn't miss me as long as I got home before they did.

The last time I'd come to Kurtzburg had been late in the evening, and I'd had to take a bus into the city. This time, Doctor Nocturne's daughter was supposed to pick me up at the cemetery. She had taken over as Kurtzburg's resident superhero since her dad had gone into semiretirement, so technically, her name was *also* Doctor Nocturne, which could get confusing.

I began to get a little uneasy as I neared the cemetery

exit. The streetlights came on, flashing dimly a few times first, as if trying to make up their minds whether they were up for the task that evening. Then the sun disappeared, but there was still no sign of Doctor Nocturne.

Kurtzburg hadn't exactly used up prime real estate when the town had decided where to stick the cemetery, and I didn't like being alone there. I slunk back toward the shadows of the willow trees, shivering, partly from nerves and partly from the cold. A hooded sweatshirt and jeans might be fine for December in Kanigher Falls, but they weren't enough for the icy breezes off Kurtzburg's Gerber Bay.

"Don't you have a heavier coat?" a voice called from behind me. I spun to see Stephanie in a blue suit and cape that matched her father's Doctor Nocturne outfit. "Why do you always sneak up on me like that?" I demanded.

"Because it's always funny to watch you react like that," she replied with a laugh.

"Where have you been? I've been waiting. Okay, I've probably only been waiting about nine minutes, but it seemed a lot longer. I thought you'd be here waiting for me."

"The sun was still up," she said with a shrug. "I'm Doctor Nocturne, not Doctor It's-Almost-Sunset-

That's-Close-Enough. I thought you were supposed to know all about superheroes. Isn't that how you got this job?"

It was well-known that Doctor Nocturne was never seen in uniform in the daylight, but I didn't see why this should stop Stephanie or her dad from coming to pick me up dressed as an ordinary citizen.

She ended the discussion by tossing me a helmet and waving me toward her motorcycle. It was a smaller, quicker one than her father's, and it didn't have a sidecar. I'd forgotten how much more difficult this made not falling off as we tore through the city.

The streets of Kurtzburg were cracked and worn, which would have made for a stomach-jarring ride at normal speeds and was practically vomit-inducing at a hundred miles per hour. Stephanie took corners so fast that the motorcycle leaned to the left until we were almost parallel to the ground. The asphalt brushed my shoulder and I thought I was about to be yanked off the motorcycle, but Stephanie cranked the throttle just in time to straighten us up.

She whipped the motorcycle through a cave entrance and revved the engine until my head went light because all the blood was being pushed to the back of my brain.

Then she sped toward the wide chasm that separated her dad's underground fortress from the outside world, and the bike soared over the gap.

This wasn't the first time I'd been inside Doctor Nocturne's subterranean headquarters, but I was still struck speechless by it. The cave was the size of a baseball stadium, but instead of bleachers, scoreboards, and hot dog stands, there were stalagmites and stalactites, banks of computer monitors, and a small crime lab. It seemed larger than I remembered, but that might have been because it was better lit this time. Doctor Nocturne stood in a training area to the left of the pneumatic elevator shaft that led to the mansion he shared with his daughter.

"Good luck," Stephanie whispered to me before she left to patrol the streets of Kurtzburg.

I crossed a metal walkway that spanned a seemingly bottomless drop into darkness. I climbed a few steps carved into the stone to join Doctor Nocturne. The training area consisted of several old pieces of gymnastic equipment—rings suspended from the cave ceiling, a balance beam, padded flooring—and a weight bench all nestled among several stalagmites. "Where do we begin?" I asked eagerly. "Lifting weights? I've never tried those ring things, but I've seen guys do it in the Olympics, so that's a start."

Doctor Nocturne frowned and slapped a stalagmite with a slightly flattened top. It was about as big around as a roll of paper towels. "Jump up and stand here," he said. Then he walked to a chair he'd set up about ten feet away and took a seat.

The stalagmite came up to my chest. I braced my hands against the top and quickly drew them back and wiped them on my shirt, leaving faint green streaks. Because of the damp cave air, a slippery, slimy moss clung to everything.

I did my best to wipe off the flattened rock surface with my hands before I tried jumping up on top of it. I locked my elbows to keep myself up, but when I tried to swing a leg over, I lost my balance and tumbled off, landing on the opposite foot. I tried again with the same result. The third time, I got my first foot up, but when I extended that leg, I toppled forward and landed much harder on my shoulder. As I stood for a fourth attempt, I caught sight of Doctor Nocturne casually tapping away at a laptop and sipping a glass of iced tea. He showed no concern for my well-being.

Still not sure what the point of all this was, I tried

for a fifth time, my hands slipping off the peak of the stalagmite before I could even pull myself up. On the sixth try, I swung myself up and sat on the narrow base before realizing that this gave me no leverage to get my feet underneath me. I had to jump back down in defeat. On the seventh try, I fell over backward and landed on my back. The eighth attempt left me in a heap facedown on the mat.

"Can you give me some help here?" I finally appealed to Doctor Nocturne.

"When you fall, try to land flat," he shouted back. "It'll keep us from having to explain how you broke your arm to your parents." That advice was the only help I would get all evening.

Around the twentieth attempt, I managed to get both feet up on the tiny platform, but as soon as I extended my legs to stand, I toppled forward. With nothing to grab to break my fall, I had no choice but to try to land flat on my stomach, knocking all the wind out of my lungs. This went on for more than an hour, with me falling on various body parts that hadn't yet been bruised while Doctor Nocturne sat and sipped his iced tea, getting up only when he needed to refill his glass.

I had naively thought training with Doctor Nocturne

would be more exciting. I'd envisioned a combination of video games, those forensic crime shows my dad liked to watch, and professional wrestling. There were dozens of computers, a crime lab, weights, and gym equipment all around me.

And all I had to work with was a slimy, slippery rock.

But I'd take what I could get. I wanted to be a good advisor to Ultraviolet, and I wanted to stay on Doctor Nocturne's good side. Finally, I managed to catch the tip of the stalagmite with both feet, which I kept planted as I pushed with my thigh muscles until I was standing up straight. I put my arms out to the sides for balance and shouted, "Okay, I'm up. What now?"

He took his time answering, draining the last of his iced tea, licking his lips, and peering down into the glass like he suspected there might be a secondary reserve of tea hidden in the bottom if he looked hard enough. "Now nothing," he answered. "You're standing. Keep standing."

What? He said to get on the stalagmite, so I got on the stalagmite. I'd assumed that was the point of this test, but now that was just step one? It didn't seem fair to me, but I didn't want to risk anything, so I took a deep breath and tried to steady myself. The edges of my shoes were hanging off the sides of the flat top of the stalagmite. I couldn't find quite enough traction to prevent them from slipping ever so slowly off the sides. My leg muscles burned from exhaustion. I don't know if I lasted a full minute, but it seemed like a lifetime. When my right knee buckled and dropped me to the mats four feet below, the pain of hitting the floor seemed like a reward. Every muscle below my chest sang thanks to me.

I mopped sweat from my face with the front of my shirt and heaved a few deep breaths. I almost wished Doctor Nocturne would laugh at me or tell me to go home or call me a quitter instead of just sitting there passively, watching me stumble and slip and nearly smash my own brains out on the floor of his cave. Again and again I leapt onto the pillar of stone and fell to the mats below.

After another twenty minutes of trying and failing, I brought myself up to a standing position and held steady. Every twitch seemed amplified, because my reflexes overcompensated, causing spasms up and down my body. Holding my muscles still was like trying to restrain a pack of dogs from chasing a stray cat.

"Getting bored yet?" Doctor Nocturne barked as he strolled calmly around the pedestal. "Do you still think this all seems like a lot of fun? Being a superhero isn't all about hidden passageways and colorful costumes and underground bases. I bet you'd rather be hanging out with your friends. I bet you're looking forward to spending Christmas with your family. But being a superhero isn't like any other job, Nate."

"But I don't even want to be a superhero," I insisted quietly. I don't think he heard me, because he never stopped talking.

"You don't get vacations or holidays or a dental plan. You want to be involved in this, it means disappointing your family and losing your friends. If you're not willing to make the sacrifices necessary—"

The roar of his daughter's motorcycle entering the cave cut him off. When he turned to watch her dismount, I was relieved to have a break.

Then I saw her arm.

Stephanie's right hand hung limply at her left side, her arm in a makeshift sling that used to be a piece of her white shirt. Doctor Nocturne darted down the stairs with a speed you don't normally see in old men with bad hips. I hurried after him, but then held back, not sure whether I could help or whether I would just get in the way.

"What happened?" Doctor Nocturne shouted.

"What's it look like?" Stephanie chuckled. "I need to change my shirt and reset this bone."

"But . . . your arm's broken," I chimed in, pointing out the obvious.

"Barely," Stephanie replied. "I hardly even feel it." She wiggled her fingers to illustrate how quickly it was healing. With her good hand, she undid the sling and straightened her arm slowly. "See? Good as new."

"Let me see," Doctor Nocturne said calmly as he reached out to examine his daughter's arm. "Who did this? Schoolboy Krush? Antisocialite? Pastor Pain?"

"I fell," she answered, looking a little embarrassed. "I was on the roof of the old Malve Industries warehouse and a ceiling beam gave out. I fell through a skylight. Stupid mistake, but I'm fine." She pulled her arm away. "Now, let me change."

"But the old Malve warehouse is solid as a rock," he said. "I've been perching up there while on patrol since before you were born."

"I know," she agreed. "I go there every night. I guess it's just getting old." She gently pushed her father away and went over to a wardrobe full of dozens of matching blue suits. Doctor Nocturne returned to the training area, where I'd been waiting while I watched the whole scene. His worried eyes and frown told me he might be rethinking his statement about sacrificing family and friends.

"As long as Stephanie's here, why don't you have her take you home?" he mumbled softly. "It's almost ten, which means it's about eight in Kanigher Falls."

I nodded agreement. When Stephanie returned, wearing a new suit and walking with a bounce in her step that would never hint that she'd shattered her arm only moments earlier, I asked for a ride to Captain Zombie's tomb. She tossed me her spare motorcycle helmet and asked how the first night had gone.

I glanced around to see if her father was listening, but he was hobbling slowly toward the elevator, his shoulders slumped. "I fell off that stupid thing about fifty times," I told her, pointing at the stalagmite.

"Only fifty?"

"And when I finally stood up on it, he didn't have anything else for me to do. So I just stood there."

"You stood up on it on your first night?" she said in surprise. "Impressive. Next thing you know, he'll be throwing the tennis balls at you."

"Tennis balls?" I gulped, but the question was lost in the roar of the engine as we shot into the night.

You Decided to Wake Up After All

The next morning, I couldn't get out of bed. There was no part of my legs that didn't ache. Just rolling over to look at the clock on my bedside table was agony. Why was I doing this to myself?

I already knew I didn't have what it took to be a super-hero, and I had never said I did. I'd certainly been able to advise Ultraviolet in the past without standing on a balance beam. It wasn't like I was going to grow up to be the Phantom Ranger. I was just a kid who liked to read comic books and thought it was cool to watch his teacher fly around saving people and smashing stuff.

But that wasn't the point. What Stephanie's comment told me was that this training was less about getting me in shape to fight crime and more about trying to get me to quit. Doctor Nocturne had never liked the idea of my hanging out with superheroes, and I was pretty sure he would love to see me give up on my own.

I strained to get out of the bed, bracing myself against the edge of my desk, and limped to the bathroom.

I'd compare the experience to wading waist-deep through a pool of lava, and going down the stairs to get breakfast was even worse. "What's your problem?" Denise asked from the couch, where she was lying while watching old black-and-white footage on the History Channel. "You look like your butt's trying to crawl inside itself and hide in your stomach."

I was arching backward in an awkward way that I probably would have found funny if it didn't hurt so much.

"Denise, go watch that somewhere else," Dad ordered before I could think of a lie to explain my silly walk. "The game's going to start in five minutes." He put a bowl of salsa and a bag of tortilla chips on the coffee table.

"But, Dad, I'm supposed to do a report on Nikita Khrushchev next month," she argued.

"There are three other TVs in this house. You don't need to watch fifty-year-old news footage in forty-two-inch high definition. Now, flip it back to the pregame show. I need to see if Bullethead is going to play." Demetrius Johnson was my dad's favorite player. Dad had tutored him when they were in college, and he claimed to have given him the nickname "Bullethead," because Johnson was so fast and hit so hard when he charged down the field headfirst.

Dad had just turned forty, though, which made Bullethead thirty-eight. That might as well be eighty for a professional football player. Every week, Dad agonized over Bullethead's various sprains, bruises, and pulls. It seemed he was more concerned about the linebacker's health than his own. During football season, Sunday dinners often featured detailed explanations of minor injuries from my mom, who was an emergency room surgeon, to help Dad understand the difference between a ligament tear and a tendon tear and how long it might take for Bullethead to get back on the field.

"Bullethead practiced on Friday and is listed as probable. He'll play," Denise informed Dad, which made him smile. "Not that he should. The Rhinos used their first-round draft pick last summer to take Sheffield, because they thought Johnson was going to retire. Instead, you have the future of the franchise sitting on the bench, and a relic starting at inside linebacker."

Dad had always encouraged us to be well-informed, but there were times when I was pretty sure Denise made him regret that.

My dad narrowed his eyes at her. "Just change the channel, Denise," he commanded. Then he returned to the kitchen, and I followed.

"What happened?" he asked. "You're walking like somebody stole your knees while you were sleeping."

"I exercised yesterday," I said. "I guess I overdid it."

"Ah, trying to get in better shape so you can pull up that P.E. grade? That's a good plan. Do you know what you're doing when you get back from break?"

"Uh, basketball, I think."

"Okay, then you should concentrate on your balance and your leg strength."

"Yeah," I said, gently massaging my thighs. "I'll have to do that."

"I can show you a few exercises if you want. Back when I was tutoring Bullethead, he taught me—"

"I think they're playing the theme music," I interrupted, pointing toward the living room.

He stopped talking and craned his neck toward the TV. Then he grabbed a can of soda and his glass and left for the living room without another word.

I stepped into the pantry for a box of cereal and emerged to find my mother coming in from the garage. She peered around cautiously, which meant she'd been shopping for presents and was making sure the coast was clear before bringing them in.

"Oh, so you decided to wake up after all," she said with mock surprise. "What did you guys do last night? When we got home from your dad's party, you were passed out, dead to the world."

"Um, Teddy and I are working out over the break. You know, so maybe Coach Howard won't yell at us so much. That's probably where I'll be tonight, too."

"Make sure you tell your dad, because I'm working a night shift at the hospital."

She paused and watched me get the milk from the refrigerator. "What did you do to your legs? You look like a baby ostrich learning how to walk."

"I guess I overdid it exercising yesterday," I replied.

"Well, be careful. Coach Howard will really yell if you have to be excused from gym because of an injury."

"What do you mean?" I asked, suddenly panicked that my cover had been blown. "How would I get hurt?"

"With you and Teddy, who knows?" she replied with a shrug. "Just promise me you won't do anything stupid, like jumping off the roof pretending you're the Astronaut and Starshiner."

She meant Shiningstar and Astro, from one of my favorite comics, but I didn't bother to correct her. "That was three years ago," I argued with a groan.

"Two years, eight months . . . and I'm too tired to figure out the days," she said, correcting me. "I have to go take a nap if I'm going to pull an all-nighter."

"If I ever figure out how to travel back in time," I began, "I'm going to go back to two years and eight months ago and tell myself, 'Don't jump off that roof! Your arm will heal in a couple weeks, but you'll have to listen to Mom talk about it for the rest of your life.'"

"If you figure out how to time travel, why don't you come back before you were born and warn me about the son I'm going to have?" she asked with a sarcastic smile. Then she shuffled into the living room to kiss my dad before heading upstairs to bed.

I took my cereal into the den so I could skim NotSoHeroic.com for new articles, but it hadn't been updated since Friday night. I'd already watched the videos and looked at the pictures. The only thing I hadn't read was Moonrock's warning article, so I clicked on it.

I may not be an astronomer or a NASA engineer or even a supergenius, but I still think I
know a thing or two about rocks from space.
I'm MOONROCK, people!

So listen up.

Monday night's meteor shower promises to be
a spectacular sight, but we can't overlook the
obvious danger. The streaks of light that will
zip across the sky are tiny meteors and debris
burning up in the atmosphere. The debris comes
from two large asteroids that will be passing
within five hundred miles of Earth. When the
meteors crash into the larger asteroids, the
shattered pieces of both float away and become
beautiful natural fireworks displays that only
come along every fifty years.

However, each impact also changes the
trajectory of the asteroids ever so slightly.
And because of those impacts, we don't know
whether the asteroids might change course.
They could come within a few hundred miles
of Earth. Or they might even hit Earth!

I don't want to cause any panic, but I've been
warning everyone about this for months and

no one seems to care. All I'm asking is that we have some kind of plan to deal with this in case something goes wrong. Is that so crazy?

Posted by: themoonrockz Friday 12:47 PM

There were several comments from readers of the blog, suggesting that his idea was, in fact, totally crazy.

I got up and carried my bowl to the sink, then headed upstairs to spend the next few hours in my room. I searched through old comics for superhero secret bases to give Ultraviolet some ideas until it was time to head to Kurtzburg for another fun evening of falling on my face.

On-the-Job Training

As soon as Stephanie dropped me off, I was determined to prove I was all business. I lifted myself onto the stalagmite and found my footing, but once again, Doctor Nocturne didn't seem to notice. That night, instead of sitting in his chair with a glass of iced tea, he was positioned in front of a bank of computer monitors on the opposite side of the cave.

I considered calling out to him and asking if there were any new pointless tasks I should take on, but my concentration was broken by a loud crash from across the cavern. I turned to look and lost my footing, tumbling over backward onto the mats and landing hard on my shoulder.

When I got up, Doctor Nocturne was no longer at the monitors. He was limping to the large wardrobe, mumbling under his breath as he went. One of the computer screens was now dark and shattered, the wooden head of the horse from the top of Doctor Nocturne's cane embedded in the center. Obviously, something had upset him, and if that was how he treated a plasma screen when he was angry, I didn't want to find out what he'd do to me if I wasn't training. I quickly jumped back up on the stalagmite and concentrated on my balance.

Moments later, Doctor Nocturne emerged from the wardrobe in his full uniform—blue suit, mask, cape, and all.

"Come on down from there, Nate," he said. He looked me up and down, pulled the hood of my sweatshirt over my head, and gave me another once-over. He held two items, both of which he handed to me. The first was a blue mask that fit just around the eyes. It matched his but was smaller. The other item was a well-worn, old, faded black baseball cap with a red *K* on it.

"Put these on."

I did as he ordered and started back to the stalagmites, but he gestured for me to follow him to his motorcycle, which again had the sidecar attached. The whole scene felt wrong, like we were doing something sneaky.

"I thought we were training down here tonight," I reminded him.

"I have more important things to do than watch you fall on your face all night," he countered. "Consider this on-the-job training."

Reluctantly, I climbed into the sidecar and covered my ears as the engine revved to life. Seconds later, we were blasting out of the cave and into the night air.

o o o

We pulled up in front of the Malve Industries warehouse, and Doctor Nocturne parked the bike.

"I really don't think Stephanie wanted us—"

"Does the term 'secret identity' mean nothing to you?" he barked. He hopped off the bike and headed toward the building. Then he began to climb a ladder up the side of the building.

"Sorry," I said as I followed him hesitantly. "I don't think . . . the other Doctor Nocturne would want us doing this."

He stopped climbing and I nearly slammed into him. "Did I give you the impression that I needed my daughter's permission to fight crime in my hometown?" he asked gruffly. "I have been this city's symbol of justice for almost sixty years, and no one is going to tell me that I can't investigate a crime."

He continued up the ladder and heaved himself over the edge of the roof. I stuck close to him, careful to avoid casting a shadow on the first two skylights so our silhouettes wouldn't alert anyone who might be watching from inside. As he walked, I could tell he was doing his best not to hobble on his bad hip, but with each step, the hitch seemed more noticeable.

When he reached the third skylight, which had a sheet of plywood over the glass on one side, he crouched. He surveyed the hole in the roof like a chess master scanning the board before a critical move. He held out his right hand, fingers spread wide, gesturing toward the edge of the hole. "See that broken ceiling beam? What do you notice?" he asked.

I didn't notice anything other than a broken piece of wood. "Um, it looks like it broke. Maybe it was rotten?"

"Look carefully," he urged.

"Can I get a clue?"

"Splinters."

I didn't see any splinters. If there had been any, they'd probably been swept up by the guy who had covered the skylight with the plywood. Even the broken beam itself looked like it had been sawed flat—was that what he was getting at? "The beam looks like it was cut?"

"Exactly," he said. "This was no accident. Someone was trying to kill me."

"Wait a minute. Kill *you*? Steph—the other Doctor Nocturne's the one who fell through the skylight."

"Yes, but whoever did this didn't know that's who would be on patrol. He must have thought it would be me." He pointed at the cut end of the ceiling beam. "Who do you think could cut a beam like that?"

"Uh . . ." I racked my brain. "Snicker-Snack's got swords. So does Colonel Blaydes. Sawhorse?" The fact was anybody with a circular saw could have done it. The beam was just a two-by-four.

"This is the work of my archenemy, Red Malice," Doctor Nocturne insisted.

That seemed doubtful to me. Red Malice was a Russian supervillain from the fifties and sixties, one of the biggest of his time, given the hostilities between the United States and the Soviet Union. He was considered a hero in his homeland because he hated everything about America. Even though it had happened decades before I was born, I'd heard about the time he'd taken the New York Stock Exchange hostage with an army of performing circus bears. His famous rivalry with Doctor Nocturne had started when he'd tried to steal the baseballs for the 1956 World Series games in Kurtzburg.

But after the Soviet Union crumbled in the early 1990s, he had pretty much retired. There was no reason for him to pop up now. "Red Malice? If he's still alive, he'd probably be, like, a hundred years old," I said.

Doctor Nocturne slowly turned to look at me with a frown, prompting me to recall that he was over ninety years old himself.

"I mean, but you're . . . He can't be . . ." I decided shutting up might be the best option. Fortunately, the awkwardness was interrupted by the wail of a police car siren in the distance. Doctor Nocturne leapt up, wincing and holding his hip for a split second. If he was in any pain, you would never have guessed it from the way he dashed to the corner of the roof.

He looked like he was about to leap for a fire escape on the next building when a voice called to him from behind us. "Dad! Where are you going?"

He stopped and pivoted in a blur, instinctively raising his fists. When he saw that it was his daughter, wearing a matching blue suit, cape, and fedora, he lowered them only slightly.

"What are you guys doing up here?" she asked. "I thought you were training in the cave."

"We were investigating this—" I started before Doctor Nocturne cut me off.

"My sources told me the Mortician was bringing in a shipment of counterfeit bills tonight."

"Yeah, I know," Stephanie replied. "You and I have the same sources, remember? I have it all under control." She pointed to a ship unloading a few piers away. "Been watching her all night. Police are already on their way. Figure it should be wrapped up in about ten more minutes."

Doctor Nocturne bit into his lower lip as he watched the ship.

"I can't believe you brought Nate out here," she said, changing the subject.

"Hey," I protested. "Secret identities."

"Fine, what do you want me to call you? *Nocturnal Boy? Kid Nighttime?*" she asked, punching each name with a sarcastic tone.

"I guess Nate's okay," I conceded.

"And, Dad, where is your cane?" she asked, turning her attention back to him.

"I'm fine without that thing," he grumbled.

"No, you're really not," she sighed. "And if you try to jump from one building to another on a bad hip, you'll be lucky if a cane is all you need."

Her father reluctantly backed down. "Come on, boy," he said to me. "Let's head back to the cave." He started toward the ladder and I followed, but Stephanie grabbed me by the shoulder.

"Nate, I know he's supposed to be taking care of you, but you're going to have to keep an eye on him, too," she said softly. "Keep him out of trouble, okay?"

I nodded.

"And make sure he uses his cane."

My mind flashed back to the broken computer monitor with the top of his cane embedded in it. "Oh, don't worry," I told her. "He's definitely using it."

I said good-bye and rushed across the roof to where Doctor Nocturne was struggling to get his stiff leg over the side of the building and onto the ladder's rungs. I watched for a few seconds before speaking up.

"Would you like some help?" I offered.

Doctor Nocturne's eyes were as hard as ever, but his face softened a bit.

"Yes, please," he admitted gruffly.

A Regular Guy,
Just Like You

When we got back to the cave, the silence was deafening. Doctor Nocturne hadn't said a word during the entire ride, and I didn't think it was only because I wouldn't have heard him over the roar of his motorcycle.

He killed the engine and limped up to the bank of computers near the pneumatic elevators, then dropped himself heavily into the high-backed leather chair that faced away from the flashing monitors. He tossed his hat weakly onto the black desk beside him and peeled off his small blue mask with a long, defeated sigh.

There was no clear indication of what I should say or do. I considered perching on the stalagmites and hopscotching between them. I assumed I would fall a few times, and maybe that would get him fired up enough to yell at me. Yelling—believe it or not—was preferable to the silence, maybe only because I'd gotten used to the yelling. The silence was unpredictable.

I started for the old gym equipment, but Doctor Nocturne growled, "Nate! Come here."

I scurried up the stone steps to the computer alcove. Doctor Nocturne was slumped low in his chair.

"Yes?" I asked hesitantly.

"I'm starting to question this whole training idea."

I held my breath, knowing that what he said next would be one of two things. He might declare I'd learned so much in two nights that he was already giving me the Doctor Nocturne seal of approval. Or, more likely, he was tired of waiting for me to quit on him and was going to drop the ax himself.

"My daughter, the Phantom Ranger, and a few others seem to think I'm too old to be a superhero just because this hip isn't healing up the way it used to. I've been trying to tell them that's because they won't let me get back out there and prove myself. Just sitting around in a dusty old mansion isn't helping anything. Hanging out down here all night is only making my hip stiffen up. Look at what happened tonight."

"Wait a minute," I interrupted. "Are you blaming me for something?"

"No," he replied, hedging. "'Blame' isn't the right word. You're coming along nicely, but I don't have time to play. There is a criminal mastermind out there with a target on me. You don't know Red Malice—"

"Actually, I know a lot about Red Malice," I protested. "He was a soldier in the Soviet Army during World War Two who was given enhanced abilities, strength, agility, stuff like that. He also used a weapon called the Hammersickle—"

Doctor Nocturne held up a hand to silence me.

"But you've never seen him in action," he said. "I fought him most of my adult life, and I know that if he's got it in for me, he's not gonna stop until he thinks he has me."

Doctor Nocturne's conclusion didn't make any sense to me, and I wanted to tell him so. The more I thought about it, the more likely it seemed that the beam had broken on its own and someone had trimmed the splintered ends with a saw afterward. And even if it had been sabotage, why, in a world full of supervillains, would he jump to the conclusion that an old man who had disappeared twenty years earlier had done it?

It sounded to me like he'd been sitting around feeling sorry for himself for so long that he actually *wished* some old nemesis was hunting him down. I guess when you've spent sixty years fighting evil, even having someone try to kill you is better than sitting home alone.

"Let me call my daughter and get you a ride back to the cemetery." He spun his chair around and began pushing buttons on one of the computer consoles.

I suppose I should have been grateful. I could spend the rest of my vacation hanging out with my friends, getting a decent night's sleep, and letting the constant ache in my muscles fade away. But I'd spent too much time and invested too much effort to be dismissed just because this old man had been embarrassed by his daughter. I had something to prove, maybe not to Doctor Nocturne—I doubted he'd acknowledge it even if I did—but to Ultraviolet, to Phantom Ranger, and to myself.

"I'd rather you didn't do that," I said.

He didn't respond.

"You said I had to get this training or I couldn't help Ultraviolet anymore," I continued. "You may not see it, but I know Ultraviolet is a better superhero with me helping her than without me."

He continued to stare at the monitors before him, showing no reaction to my words.

"So, um . . . I'm not leaving," I insisted. "I'll be balancing over there if you need me."

He spun in his chair and glared at me so hard I thought his eyes might burst into flames.

"Nate!" he said sharply. "I'm not asking you. Fun and games are over."

A voice echoed through the cavern: "Oh, there's always time for fun and games."

The cave was so, well, *cavernous* that it was hard to tell where the voice was coming from. It seemed to echo off every surface. But then I saw a glint of gold near the mouth of the tunnel that led to the cave entrance.

A moment later, the glint of gold became a shiny helmet with three blue metal fins and a mirrored visor. I couldn't believe what I was seeing.

It was the Phantom Ranger.

"Sounds like training is going about as well as I expected," he said with a chuckle. "I heard you guys had a field trip tonight."

"Now's really not a good time, Ranger," Doctor Nocturne grumbled.

"Oh, don't let me get in the way," Phantom Ranger replied. "I just wanted to see how things are going." He took a few steps toward me and smiled.

I could see my wide-eyed, stupid expression reflected in his visor. I tried to snap out of it.

"Have you been doing the stalagmite thing?" he asked.

I nodded. "Y-y-yes, sir."

The Phantom Ranger was here. Right in front of me! My favorite superhero of all time! Heck, he was my mom's favorite superhero. My grandmother didn't even know any superheroes and he was probably her favorite, too.

"Calm down, Nate. I'm just like you. I mean, a regular guy," he assured me.

But that was what made Phantom Ranger so intimidating. Among the world's greatest superheroes, only one was a "regular guy," without any superpowers. With his cunning, wit, and a limitless supply of high-tech gadgets, Phantom Ranger held his own against supervillains like Devast-8, Wintertyrant, and Colosso.

"Did you get to the part where he throws the tennis balls at you?" he asked me.

"Why does everyone keep asking that?"

Phantom Ranger laughed. "After you do it, you'll understand. It's his way of teaching you to move quickly, change direction, and remain aware of your surroundings."

"Well, it's not going to happen anytime soon," Doctor Nocturne insisted. "Red Malice is on the loose, and I'm not going to let you or my daughter tell me I'd be best put to use throwing tennis balls at this kid."

"Red Malice," the Ranger repeated. "And what makes you think Red Malice has come out of retirement?"

"The Malve warehouse," I answered. "Stephanie fell through a skylight when a ceiling beam gave out. It looked like maybe the beam had been cut."

Phantom Ranger didn't look too convinced, but then, it's hard to read someone's expression when everything above his upper lip is hidden behind a mirrored helmet.

"It *had* been cut," Doctor Nocturne insisted.

"Okay, okay," Phantom Ranger said, trying to calm Doctor Nocturne down. "Let's say Red Malice is out of retirement and out to get you. What's his next move?"

"That's what I need to find out, but I've gone from superhero to babysitter."

"Training Nate is . . . important, Doc," the Ranger said softly. "Plus, with your hip, I don't think you should be out there alone."

Doctor Nocturne glared at Phantom Ranger. "Nate, will you excuse us for a moment?" he said through gritted teeth.

I hurried away to let the two heroes argue out of earshot, and I wound up near the bank of computer monitors. There were satellite images from around the globe, newscasts in multiple languages, 3-D renderings of floor plans, spreadsheets, Internet articles, and weather radar, and my eyes jumped from one screen to the next.

Finally, my eyes fell on a tiny black-and-white portable television tuned to the local news. The TV showed aerial footage of a strip mall parking lot with a crowd gathered outside. As the helicopter swung around to the front, it captured a shot of a grocery store. The doors to the store were gone and had been replaced by the blinking tail-lights and trunk of a large, boxy, beige sedan. It was one of those huge older cars, like the landboat my grandfather used to drive until my mom finally donated it to charity and made him start riding the bus.

I stepped closer to the TV. An old man was being taken out of the store on a stretcher. While the paramedics tried to wheel him to the ambulance, the man seemed to be arguing with them. "I'm not hurt," he insisted. "Now, let me go."

"Police identified the driver as Thomas Goslin," the reporter said. "Goslin, who is eighty-two years old, managed to escape the wreckage with minor injuries. Fortunately, despite the rush of holiday shoppers out this evening, no one inside the store was hurt."

"You're not listening," Mr. Goslin continued. "Red Malice is on the loose!" The doors to the back of the ambulance slammed shut and the report returned to the anchor in the studio.

"Doctor Nocturne!" I shouted. "Doctor Nocturne!" I spun away from the TV to see both heroes looking toward me. "Do you know somebody named Tony Goslin? Or maybe Thomas or something with a 'T'?"

Both men hurried to join me at the monitor bank.

"Where did you hear about Tommy Goslin?" Doctor Nocturne demanded, scanning the monitors intently, as though I'd accessed some top secret files.

"He was on the news," I told him, pointing at the little TV. "He was in a car accident and right before they put him in the ambulance, he said Red Malice's name."

"Well," the Phantom Ranger said softly, "I guess now we know what his next move was."

"I told you," Doctor Nocturne said. "I told you and you didn't believe me."

"I didn't say I didn't believe you. I just said to take Nate with you. You could use a sidekick."

I pulled my mask from the pocket of my sweatshirt.

"Actually, I prefer to be called an advisor."

Doctor Noclingtonson, I Presume?

Wearing a uniform and a mask can be very effective when you're dealing with criminals in a dark alley, but with hospital administrators, a more straightforward approach is better. I slipped the mask into the pocket of my hoodie and approached the admitting desk with a smile, identifying myself as Tommy Goslin and asking if my grandpa had been brought in.

"I told you I don't need X-rays!" someone with an angry, ragged voice hollered from the emergency room, prompting the admitting nurse to take a deep breath. She tilted her head toward the sound as if to say that "Grandpa" had answered the question for her.

I shrugged sheepishly. "That sounds like my gramps."

She showed me to his room, where the old man sat talking to two police officers. His round belly and white

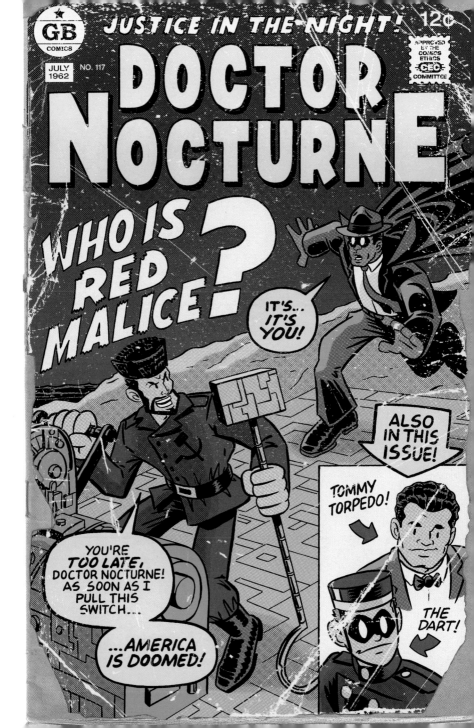

DOOM HANGS ABOVE OUR VERY HEADS! FROM *DOCTOR NOCTURNE'S* PAST COMES HIS NEW ARCHNEMESIS, *RED MALICE,* THE EASTERN BLOC BADDIE DETERMINED TO BRING THE AMERICAN DREAM *CRASHING DOWN* IN...

"THE RUSSIAN REVELATION"

SCRIPT BY *JAZZY JAKE BELL*   ART BY *CRAZY CHRIS GIARRUSSO*

JUST WHAT ARE WE *UP* AGAINST, DOC?

THE ANSWER TO *THAT* QUESTION MAY LIE *TWENTY YEARS* IN DOCTOR NOCTURNE'S *PAST...*

POLAND, 1942.

JUST WHAT ARE WE *UP* AGAINST, LIEUTENANT?

IT LOOKS LIKE MOST OF THE *GERMAN FIFTH INFANTRY DIVISION* AND MAYBE A *PANZER* OR TWO.

AND WE'RE OUT OF *AMMO.*

BOOM! BLAM!

BANG!

RAT-A-TAT-A-TAT-A-TAT-A-TA!

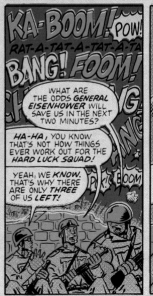

KA-BOOM! POW!

RAT-A-TAT-A-TAT-A-TA

BANG! FOOM!

WHAT ARE THE ODDS *GENERAL EISENHOWER* WILL SAVE US IN THE NEXT TWO MINUTES?

HA-HA, YOU KNOW THAT'S NOT HOW THINGS EVER WORK OUT FOR THE *HARD LUCK SQUAD!*

YEAH, WE *KNOW.* THAT'S WHY THERE ARE ONLY *THREE* OF US *LEFT!*

KLANG!

THE THREE OF *US* ARE LEFT BECAUSE WE'VE NEVER FOUND A SITUATION WE COULDN'T *FIGHT OUR WAY OUT OF!*

THAT'S *RIGHT.* THE ARMY MAY NOT GIVE US ENOUGH *BULLETS,* BUT AT LEAST THEY GAVE US *SUPERPOWERS!*

SMASH

HEY FELLAS-- YOU *HEAR* THAT?

POW

IT IS SAFE TO COME OUT NOW, MY LITTLE FRIENDS.

OR *NOT SO LITTLE FRIENDS*, I SUPPOSE!

WHEN MY COMMANDERS TOLD ME THE *HARD LUCK SQUAD* WAS IN POLAND, I HAD TO SEE FOR MYSELF.

LOOKS LIKE I CAME AT *JUST THE RIGHT TIME.*

UNH...

GUHH...

GNH...

UGH...

AND YOU ARE?

THE WORKERS OF GLORIOUS *SOVIET UNION* KNOW ME AS *COMRADE ONE.*

WE DON'T SEE MANY *AMERICANS* ON *THIS SIDE* OF THE WAR.

DO I EVEN NEED TO GUESS WHY YOU ARE HERE?

THE HARD LUCK SQUAD'S MISSION WAS TO FIND AND DESTROY A *SECRET PROJECT* DEVELOPED BY *AXIS SCIENTISTS...* AND *COMRADE ONE* KNEW EXACTLY WHERE TO FIND IT.

WHAT IS *THAT?*

THEY CALL IT A *TRACTOR BEAM...*

"...FOR NOW, THEY ARE STILL *EXPERIMENTING.* THE POWER IS VERY WEAK, BUT WITH A *GREATER* POWER SOURCE, IT COULD PULL OUR PLANES *RIGHT OUT OF THE SKY!* GERMANY WOULD BE *UNTOUCHABLE* FROM THE AIR."

AND THAT IS IF THEY ONLY USE IT FOR *DEFENSE.*

THERE IS THE CHANCE IT COULD ALSO BE USED AS A *WEAPON.*

THEN WE STRIKE *NOW.*

JUST THE *FOUR* OF US?

WELL...

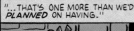
"...THAT'S ONE MORE THAN WE'D *PLANNED* ON HAVING."

KNOCK KNOCK

WER IST-?

KRAKABOOM!

THE COMBINED MIGHT OF THE *ALLIED POWERS* MOWED DOWN THE *GERMAN THREAT* THAT NIGHT, CLEARING THE PATH TO THE INFAMOUS *TRACTOR BEAM.*

THERE IT IS!

OKAY, GUYS, CHECK THE ARMORY. LET'S FIND SOME *EXPLOSIVES* AND BLOW THIS THING *SKY-HIGH!*

ACTUALLY, I HAVE A *BETTER* IDEA.

WHAT? YOU AGREED TO *HELP* US!

OUR... ..MISSION..

I AM *SORRY,* COMRADES, BUT YOU HAVE *YOUR* MISSION.. ...AND I HAVE *MINE.*

KZZZZT!

I MUST RETURN THE TRACTOR BEAM TO *MOSCOW. YOU WILL NEVER SEE ME OR THIS MACHINE AGAIN.*

TWENTY YEARS LATER...

I THOUGHT YOU SAID I'D NEVER SEE YOU OR THAT MACHINE AGAIN, *COMRADE!*

I RECOGNIZE THAT VOICE!

THE *LAST* TIME WE MET, OUR COUNTRIES WERE *ALLIES.*

BUT *NO LONGER!*

NOW I WILL DESTROY THE UNITED STATES IN A HAILSTORM OF *ASTEROIDS!*

AND THEN THE *COMMUNIST EMPIRE* WILL RULE THE WORLD!

HIGH ABOVE US ARE SEVERAL ASTEROIDS LARGE ENOUGH TO *DESTROY* THIS CONTINENT.

THIS DEVICE WILL LOCK ON TO ONE OF THOSE ASTEROIDS, AND SOON *NOTHING* WILL REMAIN OF WESTERN CIVILIZATION BUT *RUBBLE AND FLAME!*

NOT IF WE SHUT THIS THING DOWN FIRST!

ZZZZ

AARGH!

ZZZT!

I *THOUGHT* YOU MIGHT TRY SOMETHING LIKE THAT.

I'VE BEEN WAITING *TWENTY YEARS* TO PAY YOU BACK FOR WHAT YOU DID IN POLAND, *COMRADE ONE!*

I AM YOUR *COMRADE NO LONGER!*

YOU NOW FACE THE POWER OF *RED MALICE!*

SWISH

BUT LITTLE DOES RED MALICE KNOW, THEY ARE *NOT ALONE...*

...JUST BOUGHT THIS TUXEDO

AND AS THE BITTER RIVALS RENEW THEIR LONG-STANDING HOSTILITIES--

OOF!

--THE *TRACTOR BEAM* FINDS A GRIP ON AN ASTEROID AS BIG AS A *FOOTBALL STADIUM.*

BEEP!
BEEP!
BEEP!
BEEP!
BEEP!

BEEP!
BEEP!
BEEP!

HEAR *THAT?*

IT MEANS THE *DEATH OF AMERICA* IS ON ITS WAY!

AND THERE IS *NOTHING* YOU CAN DO TO STOP--

DON'T COUNT ON IT!

BUT RED MALICE'S PLAN DIDN'T COUNT ON THE INTERFERENCE OF *TOMMY TORPEDO.*

WHAT IS THIS?

I HAD A *NICE EVENING* PLANNED, RED MALICE, BUT *YOU* AND *YOUR MACHINE* HERE RUINED IT!

SO *ALLOW ME...*

...TO *RETURN...*

...THE *FAVOR!*

AND WITH THE STRENGTH OF *TEN MEN* WHO EACH POSSESS THE STRENGTH OF *TEN MEN,* TOMMY *TORPEDO* ENDS THE LATEST THREAT OF *THE RED MALICE.*

THAT'LL TEACH YOU NOT TO MESS WITH *MY* EVENING!

SMASH!

SPLASH!

WITHOUT THE PULL OF MOSCOW'S MACHINERY, THE METEOR SHOWER HARMLESSLY PASSES INTO THE COSMOS FOR ANOTHER *FIFTY YEARS.*

ONCE AGAIN, *DOCTOR NOCTURNE* AND HIS FRIENDS PROVE THE POWER OF *TEAMWORK.*

THIS ISN'T OVER, DOCTOR *NOCTURNE!*

OH, *YES* IT IS, RED MALICE!

IT WAS OVER THE DAY YOU DECIDED TO FIGHT AGAINST THE *AMERICAN WAY!*

I WILL FIGHT YOU UNTIL MY *DYING DAY,* DOCTOR NOCTURNE!

AND ON THAT DAY, *WE'LL* BE THERE TO HELP HIM DEFEAT YOU *AGAIN!*

POLICE

THE END.

beard made him look more like Santa Claus than a menace to society.

"How many times do I have to tell you?" he insisted. "My brakes must have been cut. I had no way of stopping."

"And we will investigate that, Mr. Goslin," one of the officers assured him. "However, we are citing you for not wearing corrective eyewear. You're lucky you went through the window and didn't plow into the brick wall next to it."

The police officer handed Mr. Goslin some paperwork, and the old man put on a pair of glasses that looked like two glass ashtrays connected by black plastic frames. They magnified his eyes to buglike proportions.

The officers seemed to notice me at last, and I stepped into the room.

"Hi, Grandpa!" I squealed happily, a big fake grin on my face.

"Who the—?" the old man started.

"I just got off the phone with the doctor up on Gerber Drive," I interrupted. "He wants to see you."

"This is not my grandson, and I don't have a doctor on Gerber Drive," Mr. Goslin argued. "It's been years since I've even gone over to that side of town. It's too ritzy for me. The only reason I ever go there is to visit—" Something seemed to click in his head.

"You remember, Grandpa?" I turned to the police and rolled my eyes. "He's very forgetful."

"Oh, you mean Doctor Noc—" He caught himself before blurting it out. "—lingtonson."

"Right, Grandpa. Doctor...Noclontingson wants to see you."

"Excuse me, son, but are your parents here?" one of the officers asked me.

"Nope. Just me."

"You came to the hospital by yourself at ten o'clock at night to find your grandfather?" the officer asked.

"After getting a call from Dr. Noctingbinstein, your grandfather's doctor from the 'ritzy' part of town?" the other added skeptically.

"Nockinglonton," I said, correcting him.

"Right," Mr. Goslin agreed.

The police eyed us suspiciously but didn't seem to care enough to bother catching us in our obvious lies. "Mr. Goslin, I am issuing this ticket and I am informing you that your license to drive is hereby suspended until such time as the municipal court of Kurtzburg reinstates it. Do you understand?"

Thomas Goslin nodded and signed the form given to him, holding the clipboard about an inch and a half from his face as he did. The officers left and Mr. Goslin leaned close to get a good look at me. "You're not really my grandson, are you?"

"No, I'm just working with Doctor Nocturne."

"You're not *his* grandson, are you?"

"Does he look like one of my relations?" A booming voice came from behind a curtain beside us. The curtain flew back to reveal Doctor Nocturne.

"How long have you been back there?" I asked.

"Long enough, Nockringlonstone," he grumbled. Then he turned his attention to Mr. Goslin. "What were you doing driving around when we both know you can't see past the tip of your nose?"

"I drive fine," Mr. Goslin protested stubbornly.

"Clearly. Is that why you stopped before you hit the produce section?"

"My brakes were cut!" Mr. Goslin snapped back. "I told the cops, and I'll tell you. I was pulling into a parking spot, I hit my brakes, and the car kept going. I tried to jerk the steering wheel so I'd hit the brick wall, but I wasn't fast enough."

"But if you hit the brick wall, you would have been killed," I chimed in.

Both men stared at me for a moment, then broke up

laughing. I hadn't thought that Doctor Nocturne knew how to laugh, and the sound of his laughter was more terrifying than I could have imagined.

"You didn't tell him who I am?" Mr. Goslin chuckled.

"It didn't come up," Doctor Nocturne replied.

"Kid, I'm Tommy Torpedo."

He clearly was expecting a bigger reaction than the one I gave him, which consisted mostly of a blank stare and a weak handshake.

"Tommy Torpedo?" he repeated. "Tommy Torpedo, Kurtzburg's greatest superhero?"

"Whoa!" Doctor Nocturne stopped him. "I don't know if that's senility or if you're just lying, but everyone knows Doctor Nocturne is, was, and always will be Kurtzburg's greatest hero."

"You may have had a few more years than me, but how can you hope to compete with Tommy Torpedo, man of adventure?" Tommy Torpedo boasted while flexing what might have been muscles once in the distant past. "With his bulletproof skin and the strength of ten men who each possess the strength of ten men!"

"You mean you're as strong as a hundred men?" I asked, confused.

"Where's the poetry in that?" Tommy said with a sigh.

"So that's why you weren't hurt in the accident," I said, stating the obvious.

Before we could ask about Red Malice, we were interrupted by a nurse who came in to discharge Tommy Torpedo. Doctor Nocturne held out a hand while pressing the other to his temple, and the nurse responded by paying close attention to a jar of tongue depressors long enough for him to hide behind the curtain before she could spot him.

As the nurse examined Tommy one last time, we heard a huge gust of wind in the hallway.

Tommy, the nurse, and I all turned to look at the doorway as the gust stopped. Standing there, staring at us, was a thin man who leaned on a walker. He was gripping it with white knuckles on both hands, yet he still looked as though he was about to topple over. If I'd had to guess, I would have said he was well over ninety years old, but considering the people I'd just been speaking with, I didn't dare hazard that guess. He might have been two hundred, for all I knew.

"I got here as fast as I could," he wheezed.

Old Spice and Prune Juice

After some quick thinking and double-talk, we managed to get Tommy Torpedo and our new guest out of the hospital without too many questions and without raising any obvious red flags. Unfortunately, it seemed to take forever, because every step with the old man who'd joined us was a labor. He'd heave his walker forward a few inches, then take about a dozen tiny steps to catch up to it, and then he would repeat the movements. This pattern was broken up by the occasional wheezing and coughing fit, or a stop to adjust the tubing that ran from a small oxygen tank on the leg of the walker up to his nose.

"I never expected to see you here," Doctor Nocturne told him.

"The only reason you can see me is because"—the old man took a deep, ragged breath—"because I'm letting you." He held up his right fist, showing off a ring made of blue metal. The three men laughed loudly. I had no idea what was going on.

"So, you're a superhero, too?" I asked.

"Not just a superhero, but—hhheeehhh—Kurtzburg's greatest superhero. They call me—hhheeehhh—the Dart," he said, taking my hand to shake it.

My fingers grazed the blue ring, and my legs immediately felt stronger. I felt like running, which was saying something, because in seven years of public school gym classes, I had never once had the urge to jog, much less sprint. That was when I started to notice things around me. It was like the world had turned into a movie on a DVD player and someone had pressed the slow button.

Some things didn't seem to move at all, like the nurses talking outside the hospital while on break. One was in mid-gesture during what must have been the most important part of whatever story she was telling. Other things were moving, but not like I'd ever seen them move before. A pigeon left its perch on a ledge outside one of the hospital's second-floor windows and flapped its wings, but in an impossibly slow way. A car that pulled into the hospital driveway off the main street confirmed what I'd seen from the pigeon, creeping across the parking lot in search of a space at a speed that would easily allow a snail to overtake it in a race.

When our hands separated, the world around me returned in a rush of noise and action. The nurse wrapped up her story to the amused laughter of her coworker, the pigeon picked up the pace of its flapping and headed for a tree on the other side of the parking lot, and the car found a space after only a few seconds of searching.

"What was . . . ?" I gasped, stumbling backward. The air suddenly felt thicker and more restrictive.

The Dart tapped his ring with a wide, knowing smile stretched across his weathered face. "The Ring of Mercury," he wheezed. "Gives the wearer control over—"

"You can't call yourself Kurtzburg's greatest hero when you retired to Florida thirty years ago," Tommy Torpedo argued jokingly, cutting off the Dart's explanation of whatever it was I'd experienced.

"What brings you back to town, Dart?" Doctor Nocturne asked.

"I assume the same thing that brought you here, Doc Noc," the Dart replied before taking a long breath.

Doctor Nocturne bristled. "Don't call me Doc Noc, Dart."

"I saw what happened to Tommy on the television—hhhheeeehhhh—and after Red Malice tried to kill me, I suspected—"

"Wait," Tommy Torpedo interrupted. "He got to you, too?"

Between wheezes, the Dart tried to recount his story. "Yesterday after—hhheeehhh—afternoon, I—hhheeehhh . . . Yesterday afternoon, I was walking—hhheeehhh—"

Doctor Nocturne stepped in, holding out his hands for the Dart to stop. He took a deep breath and closed his eyes. "This will be faster," he promised, though his lips didn't move.

"Yesterday afternoon was just another typically beautiful southern Florida day," the Dart's voice said directly inside my head. When he didn't have to stop to catch his breath every five words, his speech came out like a drumroll. "I honestly don't know why you two stay up here in the cold and the snow. Move down to Dillon with me and the rest—"

"Dart!" Tommy said boldly. "The doc said this would be faster! Stick to the topic."

"I was walking to the mailbox. Ruth and Earl York were out golfing. Herman Majeski was arguing with June

Webb about her cats peeing on his begonias. I swear, I've heard those two go back and forth about those pests at least a hundred times—"

"Dart!"

As he talked, my eyes went a bit blurry until images began to form. I could see the Dart inching slowly along the sidewalk at a retirement community. An older couple riding a golf cart waved to him. Another old man shouted at an old woman who was protectively holding a cat in her arms.

I wasn't sure if my imagination was doing this on its own or if this was a side effect of the bridge Doctor Nocturne had built between all our minds.

The Dart continued to narrate his story about checking his mail while I saw what he'd seen, heard what he'd heard, and smelled what he'd smelled, which was a disgusting combination of Old Spice and prune juice.

Mildred Brucker, he explained, was the newest member of the Marston Palms community, and she was having a piano delivered to her third-story condominium. The movers had built a pulley system on the roof and were squaring up the piano with the balcony when the cable suspending it made a loud twang that rang in my ears.

I watched the piano fall directly toward the Dart,

who'd been passing beneath Mildred's balcony at that moment. But just as the piano was a few feet above his head, everything slowed down, like when I had shaken his hand. The piano, which had been falling so fast it had been a blur, hung in space as though still suspended by its cable.

I didn't have long to examine it. The Dart ran out from under the piano and everything became a blur, stretching into long streaks of color that didn't stop until he was in a field. A cow to my left looked at the Dart quizzically. "I was in South Carolina," the Dart informed us. "That's about five hundred miles or so from where I started. I know because that's where I usually wind up if I take off without a real plan as to where I'm going. Straight shot north. I think I've seen that cow a couple of times before—"

"Dart, get on with it," Tommy urged.

The Dart took his time making a complete turn toward the south, lifting the walker and rocking back and forth until his feet faced the right direction. Once he was settled, the surroundings disappeared into long streaks again until, seconds later, he was on the roof of Mildred's condo, looking down on the splintered remains of the piano.

"I grabbed the end of the cable," he narrated as we

watched him do exactly that. "I knew there was no way it had just snapped like that, and sure enough, I got my proof. The cable wasn't frayed or stretched or strained in any way. There was a clean cut straight across."

The Dart's condominium complex faded away and the parking lot returned to my vision. A shiver ran through Doctor Nocturne and he leaned a little harder on his cane for a moment.

"So, Red Malice has been a busy man," Tommy Torpedo mused.

"It wouldn't be the first time he's crossed paths with all of us," Doctor Nocturne said.

"And it won't be the last," the Dart wheezed. An uncomfortable silence fell over the boisterous trio. From the looks on their faces, it seemed to me that it had just occurred to everyone that there was a good chance this would, in fact, be the last time.

"Hang on," I chimed in. "How do any of you know that Red Malice was behind what happened to you? The only common factor here is that something was cut in all three of these cases. They could have been accidents. It could have just been coincidence. Or it could have been anyone else in the world who owns a saw or a pair of bolt cutters."

The three men paused and glanced at one another.

"Still think it's Red Malice?" Tommy asked.

"Red Malice," Doctor Nocturne agreed.

"That's what I was thinking," wheezed the Dart.

"Fine," I sighed. "Then what's our next move?"

"Next move," the Dart gasped. "My feet are killing me. I want to—hhhheeeehhhh—get them in a nice soak and then go straight to bed."

"Yeah, it's almost midnight." Tommy Torpedo yawned. "A good night's sleep is in order before we launch the Torpedo!"

I could see the disappointment on Doctor Nocturne's face, but I couldn't argue. After all, if I wasn't home soon, my parents would probably start calling Teddy's house to tell me to come home.

Tommy Torpedo squeezed his rotund self into Doctor Nocturne's sidecar and held out my helmet for me.

"You're going to have to ride behind the Doc," he said.

I strapped on the helmet, jumped onto the back of the motorcycle, and gripped Doctor Nocturne's shoulders for support as we tore off toward the Kurtzburg Cemetery.

What's More Important Than Nightowl?

Once a comic is preserved in a plastic sleeve with an acid-free piece of cardboard behind it to prevent it from getting wrinkled, it is filed alphabetically and numerically in what is known among collectors as a long box. Long boxes are about three feet long and, when full, weigh around sixty pounds and hold more than two hundred comic books.

The thing is, you never take into account the volume of your collection—six long boxes containing 1,312 comics, weighing around 365 pounds—until you have to go through it, looking for images of secret bases to help a superhero come up with ideas for her own hidden lair.

Around 200 pounds into the project, I had a stack of a few dozen comic books for Ultraviolet to review.

That might be enough, but I didn't want to miss any good examples. Besides, I wanted to show her some of Warvictor's war room and, if I was going to be thorough, I had a long way to go before I hit the *W*s.

"Looking for secret headquarters?" Fiona asked from my doorway. I hadn't heard her come in, and I jumped.

"Huh?" I responded, pretending not to know what she was talking about.

"Ms. Matthews was talking about secret bases the other day. I take it she's getting one?"

What I wanted to say was "Yes! And it's awesome! There's an elevator and secret entrances, and if the computers are half as nice as the setup Doctor Nocturne has, it will be the best hideout on Earth! Oh, and guess who I met last night. Phantom Ranger!" Instead, I shrugged and pretended to be really interested in an old *Nightowl* comic.

"I get it," Fiona said. "I guess it wouldn't be a *secret* headquarters if you told everyone about it." She seemed to sense my unease and changed the subject. "Teddy'll be over in a little bit. He had some chores that he—"

"Teddy's coming, too?"

"Yeah, we figured we'd watch the *Nightowl* DVD," she said, pulling it from her jacket pocket. "Since you couldn't do it Saturday and neither of us saw you yesterday, I brought it along today."

"Well . . . I can't do it tonight, either."

Fiona looked suspicious. "Teddy and I just figured that since we're all going to watch the meteor shower tonight, we could hang out first."

I had forgotten about the meteor shower. It seemed unlikely that Mrs. Sutcliffe was going to follow up to make sure we had watched it.

"You *are* going to watch the meteor shower, right?" Fiona asked.

"I, uh . . . of course," I replied. Because of the time difference between Kurtzburg and Kanigher Falls, I'd been getting home around eight. I figured I could finish up training and then meet Teddy and Fiona for some sky gazing. "But I can't watch the DVD."

"Can't watch the DVD?" Teddy repeated as he entered the room. "What's more important than *Nightowl*?"

Fiona locked her gaze on the stack of comics I'd been pulling. "I'm guessing that Ultraviolet's sidekick here has more important things to do than spend time with his friends. Maybe if we had superpowers, he'd like us more."

"If we had superpowers, I'd like us more, too," Teddy

told Fiona. Then he turned to me. "You're hanging out with Ultraviolet? That's so cool. Is that where you were the last couple of nights?"

"I'm not hanging out with Ultraviolet," I protested. "I'm doing something else. And I can't tell you, so don't ask."

Teddy stepped forward and leaned in closer. "What are you going to be doing?"

"I just told you not to ask."

"I know. And I just said, 'What are you going to be doing?' Are you helping build the secret headquarters? I can help with that. I helped my dad build a tree house when I was seven."

"That tree house fell down when we were eight," Fiona countered.

"That was the tree's fault, not mine," Teddy said defensively. "You should try to get in on this, Fiona. Ultraviolet might need a spice rack or a step stool."

The sunlight was growing dim outside my window and I knew I had to leave for Kurtzburg soon. Before Fiona could continue the bickering, I interjected.

"I'm not helping build a secret anything," I said. "And I can't tell you what I *am* doing, either. At least not yet."

But would I ever be able to tell them? Was this what Doctor Nocturne had tried to warn me about Saturday night in the cave? Living a life of secrecy meant shutting out friends and family, and Fiona's skeptical stare was like one of the school bully Meathead McCaskill's stomach punches.

Unable to tell them any more than I already had, I apologized and said I had to leave. Fiona patted the *Nightowl* DVD in her jacket pocket and defiantly ordered Teddy to follow her back to her house.

"But I thought we couldn't watch it at your house," Teddy reminded her, but she was already halfway down the stairs and didn't seem to be listening.

"Teddy," I called, catching him just before he headed down after her.

"Yeah?"

"This might not be the best time to ask, but if my dad calls your place, can you tell him I'm there and make some excuse for why I can't come to the phone?"

He nodded slowly. "I'll tell him you're in the bathroom. And that we had burritos."

"Ew." Teddy was gross, but it could work.

Once they were gone, I hurried back to my room to grab my hoodie and Doctor Nocturne's baseball cap. The mask was still in the pocket of the sweatshirt, but I didn't put it on yet. I left a note on the kitchen counter.

Dad,

Hanging out at Teddy's. Might go to Fiona's to watch DVDs, then going to watch meteor shower at the park tonight with some kids from science class. Will be home late.

Nate

Taking my bike from the garage, I felt terrible. I hated not being able to include my friends. And I didn't like lying to my dad, either. As I rode to the cemetery, I tried to think about what Doctor Nocturne would have in store for me, hoping that would distract me from feeling guilty. Would it be another evening of standing on pillars of stone? Or would I be scaling buildings in Kurtzburg again?

I left my bike outside the mausoleum and quickly passed through, politely refusing Captain Zombie's offer to share half a chicken salad sandwich, and exiting into the Kurtzburg Cemetery. It wasn't long before I saw the single headlight of a motorcycle approach, but when it pulled up beside me, Doctor Nocturne wasn't alone.

Tommy Torpedo sat in the sidecar, his long white beard jutting out in all directions from being blown wildly by the wind. Doctor Nocturne eyed me strangely, like he was surprised to find me waiting for him.

"What's happening?" I asked as I slipped the mask out of my pocket and put it on.

"We found him," answered the Dart through raspy breaths from behind me. I jumped, startled. I'd had no idea he was there.

"Found who? Red Malice?" I asked in disbelief.

"He's living in a retirement home in Claremont," Tommy added. "We're going to pay him a little visit." He cracked the knuckles on one hand against the palm of the other.

The Dart chuckled for a moment, before he started hacking and coughing. I noticed that he was wearing a burgundy uniform jacket with brass buttons on the front, like something a bellhop would have worn in the 1930s, and a mask like mine.

"I'll meet you there!" he called as he disappeared in a streak. I stared after him, still finding it hard to believe that a man with a walker could vanish from sight in a matter of milliseconds.

"Nate, if you're coming, then let's go," Doctor Nocturne growled impatiently.

Who's This? Nightboy?
Kid Dusk?

The motorcycle eased into the entrance of Captain Zombie's crypt without any trouble, which was odd, considering every time I'd walked inside, the stairway had been no wider than the door to my bedroom. But then, who was I to question the physics of a living dead man's magical mausoleum that existed simultaneously in all the world's graveyards?

Once inside, Doctor Nocturne shut off the engine and left the motorcycle parked on the stairs. He dismounted and walked the rest of the way down the marble steps, leaning heavily on his cane for support. I followed, but Tommy stayed in the sidecar. Not only did he struggle to maneuver into and out of the seat, he confided that he found Captain Zombie "disturbing."

Captain Zombie was waiting for us at the bottom of the stairs with a wide brown grin and a wave.

"Doctor Nocturne, how nice to see you again. And who's this? Nightboy? Kid Dusk?" he asked, as though he hadn't just seen me a moment before.

"We need to get to Claremont," Doctor Nocturne ordered.

"Certainly," Captain Zombie agreed. "Can I get you something to drink while you're here? I know you're partial to iced tea, and I have a green tea I picked up from a market just outside a cemetery in the Zhejiang Province of China."

I noticed that Captain Zombie already had glasses out, the ice bucket filled, and a bowl of snacks on the silver tray on the bar. Also, half of his chicken salad sandwich was missing.

"Oh, where are my manners?" Captain Zombie said with a start. He stepped aside to let us see he had guests in his living room. "Doctor Nocturne, these are my friends Fiona and Teddy."

They'd been silent, and it was no wonder. Their mouths hung open and they appeared to have forgotten how to blink. My best friends sat on Captain Zombie's comfortable chairs, staring at me in disbelief. I managed a weak wave, but nothing more before Doctor Nocturne leaned in close.

"What are they doing here?" he snapped at me.

"I have no idea!" I replied.

"Why didn't you tell us?" Fiona whispered, but I didn't dare answer her.

"I made it very clear that you were not to tell your friends about this," Doctor Nocturne reminded me, as if I needed reminding.

"Have you beaten up any bad guys?" Teddy asked with wide eyes. "Do you have any powers? Whoa! Did you develop powers? Is that why you were acting weird the last few days? I can't believe you would develop superpowers and not tell your best friend! What are your powers? Can you fly?"

I felt Doctor Nocturne's angry stare on me, so I could only wave my hands at Teddy in a plea for him to stop asking questions.

"I don't have time for this," Doctor Nocturne barked. "Claremont, Zombie! Tommy Torpedo's waiting upstairs, and the Dart is probably already there."

Captain Zombie leaned around Doctor Nocturne and called up the stairs, "Hello, Tommy. Can I get you something to drink?"

"N-no, thanks," came the timid response.

"Enough with the niceties, Zombie," Doctor Nocturne insisted. "Red Malice is hunting me. He's hunting my friends. I need to get to the Cole Campus for the Aged and Infirm in Claremont. *Right now.*"

"Red Malice?" Captain Zombie said, looking surprised. "Didn't he retire more than a decade ago?"

"When he was in his prime, he was the most dangerous enemy I'd ever known," Doctor Nocturne said dramatically. "In the last two days, he's nearly killed three of the greatest superheroes of all time." That description seemed a little generous in my opinion, and Captain Zombie's expression seemed to indicate that he agreed with me.

"If this is really as bad as you say, don't you think you should tell Doc—well, *the other* Doctor Nocturne about it?" Captain Zombie asked.

Doctor Nocturne reacted as if Captain Zombie had just slapped him across the face. He tightened his jaw into an even fiercer scowl. "This is my business, Zombie. She has enough on her plate already."

I was thankful Captain Zombie had raised the question that had been brewing in the back of my mind since Tommy Torpedo had first claimed that his brakes had been sabotaged. I couldn't count the number of times

I'd listened to my dad curse elderly drivers who failed to signal or drove too slow or switched lanes without warning. And considering that the lenses in Tommy's glasses appeared to have come off the Hubble Space Telescope, I wasn't sure I bought his story.

The same went for Doctor Nocturne's insistence that the Malve warehouse roof had been sabotaged, and for the Dart's suspicion that the piano hadn't just fallen, but had been deliberately dropped. That all three had immediately suspected Red Malice meant either that Red Malice was a strategic criminal genius, or that they all were simply jumping to the same conclusion without any real evidence.

Even if he was right and this wasn't just some wild-goose chase based on a lie—or, optimistically, a misperception— from an old superhero like I thought it was, there was no need to be rude to Captain Zombie. And if there really was someone hunting a group of superheroes who hadn't been active since the 1970s, and that person was willing to drop a piano on an old man and cut another's brake lines, maybe we should be calling in the likes of Ultraviolet instead of leaving it up to the Geriatric Squad.

"Just promise me that you'll let Na—" Captain Zombie hung on my name, clearly realizing that even though my true identity was the worst-kept secret in the room, superhero code would deem it impolite to out me without my permission. "Promise me that you'll let your assistant call in . . . the other Doctor Nocturne should he decide it's . . . necessary."

"Nate's not going with us," Doctor Nocturne said flatly. "We had a deal, and he broke it. He can go home."

With not a thread of my secret identity remaining, I peeled off my mask. "I didn't tell them anything," I argued, but Doctor Nocturne wasn't listening.

"We have work to do," Doctor Nocturne replied harshly. "This is no place for kids."

"Fine," Captain Zombie agreed with a sigh. He closed his eyes as though he was concentrating very hard. "There's a private cemetery about nine miles from the Cole Campus for the Aged and Infirm. That's as close as I can get you."

"That'll work," Doctor Nocturne said. He wheeled around and whistled to Tommy Torpedo as he hobbled upstairs to the motorcycle. We heard the engine roar and the tires squeal, and then we were left in silence.

No One Sneaks Up on the Dart

I sat in one of Captain Zombie's leather chairs with my hands tucked between my knees and my eyes on the floor, purposely avoiding my friends' gazes.

"What's wrong with you guys? It's quiet like a tomb in here." Captain Zombie laughed as he brought around some sodas on a tray.

We didn't respond.

"*Dead* silent," he added, milking his joke.

Fiona began to interrogate me. "Yesterday, when I called your house to talk to you about the new issue of *Sisteroid* and you weren't home, this is what you were doing?"

"Nobody cares about a girls' comic like *Sisteroid*," Teddy interjected. "Let's stick to the important issues. Dude, can you take me flying? Just real quick. Like, let's go outside and you can fly me around the cemetery just one time. It'll take one minute. No, two. All right, five, tops. Seriously, Nate, please take me flying for five minutes and I'll never ask you for anything again. It can be my Christmas present."

"I couldn't tell you guys," I explained, ignoring Teddy. "He made me promise to keep my training a secret."

"Training?" Fiona probed. "What kind of training?"

"Superhero training. Or sidekick training. I don't even know what it was supposed to be. I told him I was just an advisor, but he said if I wanted to help Ultraviolet, I needed to learn to handle myself."

"You?" she asked skeptically. "*You* get to train to be a superhero—or a sidekick? I guess that's because *you* hit Coldsnap with that thermos of coffee? Or because *you* figured out that he was hiding in the old sauerkraut factory?" Her point wasn't lost on me, since Teddy had been the one to get the jump on Coldsnap while I was writhing on the ground in pain, and she had been responsible for figuring out the location of the supervillain's secret hideout.

"Or because *you* helped Ultraviolet defeat Dr. Malcontent?" Teddy added.

"Wait," Fiona said, exasperated. "He actually did do that."

"I know; that's why — oh, I see what you're doing," Teddy said. "Sorry to interrupt."

"It seems to me your superhero friends like you so much because of some of the things your regular old friends do," Fiona said accusingly. "And then you don't even bother to tell us? What are you going to do when you meet Phantom Ranger? Keep it to yourself—"

"I actually met Phantom Ranger last night," I admitted. "It was . . . one of the cooler things I've ever done."

Teddy gasped and shot his hand up to cover his mouth in embarrassment.

"Okay, let me just step in for a moment," Captain Zombie said. "Let's calm down and remember we're all friends, right?"

The three of us exchanged glances.

"First off, Fiona, do you really think Nate would keep his learning how to be a superhero a secret if it was up to him? Or do you think he'd be boring you with every single detail until you begged him to shut up?"

Fiona nodded sheepishly, clearly realizing that Captain Zombie was right. I wasn't exactly known for finding it easy to keep my mouth shut.

"And, Nate, how are you enjoying life as Doctor Nocturne's ideal superhero?" he asked me in a much softer tone, placing a comforting bony hand on my shoulder. "I'm guessing he told you how important it is to be willing to sacrifice family and friends for the good of justice or truth or whatever."

I nodded.

"Have you noticed that's coming from a man who raised his own daughter to be a superhero, just like him? And that same man is, right now, teaming up with friends he's had since the Eisenhower administration. Does that sound like someone who's given up on friends and family?"

I shrugged. He did have a point.

"Don't get me wrong," Captain Zombie continued. "Doctor Nocturne is noble and brave and everything you could want from a hero, and you'll have a hard time finding a superhero alive today who doesn't owe him something. But that doesn't mean he knows everything. He's also bitter and rude and reluctant to acknowledge the contributions of others, whether they're twelve-year-olds who've faced down multiple supervillains or a zombie superhero who transports him from one end of the country to the other whenever he asks."

He finished his speech and turned his attention to

Teddy. "And, Teddy, Nate doesn't know how to fly," he said bluntly. "Quit bugging him about it."

Teddy dropped his head in disappointment.

"I'm sorry I didn't tell you guys," I managed to say. "I wanted to. Heck, I was going to learn how to be a superhero. Even if I never used my training, it was pretty cool...though you'd be surprised how boring it can be."

"I'm sorry I got mad at you," Fiona said.

"I'm sorry you can't fly, Nate," Teddy added.

"Yeah, yeah, you're all sorry," Captain Zombie said. "Now, Nate, Stephanie asked me to remind you to make sure Doc Noc is using his cane and that he doesn't overwork himself, okay? And didn't Phantom Ranger make Doctor Nocturne promise to take you along on this investigation?" he reminded me. "At least, that's what the Ranger told me. Just think of this as me helping Doc Noc keep his promise."

"What do you mean?" I asked, confused.

"If you hurry, you should be able to get to the old folks' home before Tommy and the Doctor," he told us, pointing up the stairs.

"You said the closest cemetery was nine miles away," Fiona replied.

"True," Captain Zombie agreed. "I *did* say that, though

in fact that private cemetery's more like fifteen miles away. The truth is you're going to a rather . . . low-budget old-age home. There's a cemetery across the street from that dump." He leaned toward me and winked his dry, scaly eye.

"Well, then why did you send him to the wrong place?" I asked.

Captain Zombie shrugged as if the answer was obvious. "He was being a jerk. I figured a fifteen-mile drive might make him think about being a little more polite next time."

When Captain Zombie smiled, it was contagious. After a few seconds of imagining Doctor Nocturne and Tommy Torpedo tearing along miles of unnecessary roads, I couldn't help laughing, and my friends joined in. "You know, I could really use your help," I told Teddy and Fiona.

"Well," Fiona said with a shrug, "I did have a pretty intense game of cribbage scheduled with Captain Zombie."

"Get going," he said, encouraging us. "The way Doctor Nocturne drives, fifteen miles won't take him too long."

We hurried up the stairs and out into a poorly kept

graveyard in Southern California. "Did anyone think maybe we should have asked for directions?" Teddy said.

"I don't think that's going to be a problem," Fiona declared, pointing behind us.

Teddy and I turned to face a large brick-and-cement building across the street. The only thing that kept it from looking condemned were a few dim lights illuminating the windows, many of which were broken. I wondered whether they'd been broken by kids throwing rocks from the outside or by residents trying to get out from the inside.

As soon as we stepped out of the cemetery, there was a blast of wind from down the street. Then something blew past us at unbelievable speed, and I found myself on my back in the grass. I sat up and spotted my friends, both pinned by a walker to the fence surrounding the Cole Campus for the Aged and Infirm. An old man wearing a bellhop's uniform and an oxygen tube in his nose loomed over them.

"Didn't expect to see me tonight, did you—hhheeehhh?" the Dart yelled, gasping for breath. Teddy and Fiona struggled against the walker, looks of pure panic on their faces.

"Dart, no!" I shouted over their terrified screams. "They're friends!"

The Dart turned and squinted at me in the darkness. "Who's that? Don't think you can sneak up on the Dart!"

"It's Nate. From the hospital." I stepped forward slowly with my hands out.

"Nate?" he asked, looking confused. "Where are Doc Noc and Tommy?"

"They're on their way," I answered. "We took a shortcut."

He sighed in relief and inhaled deeply from the oxygen tube. "I thought you were henchmen—hhheeeehhh—or worse."

"Can you let us go now?" Fiona whispered, her voice hoarse from screaming.

"Oops, sorry about that," the Dart said, releasing them and nearly toppling over backward before he steadied the walker and caught himself. "I'm just a little wound up. I haven't done this in thirty years. Guess I'm kind of rusty."

We stared across the street at the decrepit building, not sure what to expect. "Is he in there?" I asked.

"I don't know," the Dart said. "I think we should wait for the others and go in together."

I nodded, but Fiona disagreed. "You can't go charging in there, pinning people to walls with your walker and reading people's minds, or whatever it is Doctor Nocturne does. And I don't know who Tommy Torpedo is, but his name doesn't sound like someone who's all about subtlety. You'll give someone a heart attack."

"Yeah. Maybe yourself," Teddy added under his breath.

"She has a point. That uniform kind of stands out," I noted, indicating his outfit.

"Still fits. I guarantee you Tommy—hhheeeehhh—Torpedo can't say that. Don't get much chance to wear the old togs anymore—hhheeeehhh—so I thought I should take advantage of the opportunity."

We had to find out for certain what we were dealing with, and I knew the perfect way to get the reconnaissance we needed. "Wait out here," I told my friends and the Dart. "This worked before."

The lobby of the nursing home smelled of dead flowers and ointments, but I tried not to let that affect me as I strode up to the nurse behind the reception desk.

"Excuse me," I said. "I'm wondering if my grandpa is here."

She looked through the thick pane of glass with complete disinterest. "What's your grandfather's name?"

I froze. "Grandpa . . ." I didn't know Red Malice's real name. Without thinking, I babbled, "Grandpa Red . . ."

"Red Malice?" she asked, perking up nervously. "You're Yuri's grandson?"

"Yes, can you tell me what room he's in?"

The nurse held up a finger to ask for a moment. She slipped away from the desk and came back with a man in a white short-sleeved dress shirt and a tie. He swallowed nervously.

"Hello, I'm George Sanchez, the home administrator," he said. His forced smile looked even more desperate under the dim greenish glow of the fluorescent lights in the hallway. "I'm afraid we have some bad news. We didn't have any contact information for Yuri's next of kin, so we weren't sure who to call when this happened—"

"When what happened?"

"Two months ago, your grandfather was diagnosed with cancer. A terminal case. He left us about a week and a half ago." He tried to console me. "I'm sorry, but we lost him."

A Booby Trap in Every
Can of Borscht

"What are you doing here?" Doctor Nocturne growled as he burst through the front doors of the old folks' home, Tommy Torpedo, the Dart, Teddy, and Fiona right behind him.

"Um, we took a shortcut," I replied.

"I told you to go home."

I held up a hand to quiet him down and hoped he would realize he was making a scene in front of strangers, the exact scene I'd hoped to avoid by coming in alone. "I just asked them about Red Malice," I said softly. "He's dead."

"What?" Doctor Nocturne said.

"What?" Tommy Torpedo said.

"What?" the Dart said.

"What?" Mr. Sanchez said, waving his arms in front of him. "Wha—no, no, no."

"You said you lost him," I reminded him.

"Right," Mr. Sanchez replied. "Meaning we don't know where he is."

"What!" Doctor Nocturne repeated.

"Last Thursday, Mr. Maximov didn't come to dinner," Mr. Sanchez explained. "We've had several instances of residents, um, wandering off the property. Usually we find them within a day or two, so we didn't make a big deal out of it." He smiled nervously, looking like he expected to be fired, or sued, or punched in the face, or all three.

"Where's his room?" Doctor Nocturne asked Mr. Sanchez.

"Oh, I'm afraid I can't tell you that unless you're family."

Doctor Nocturne took a deep breath, placed one hand to his temple, held the other out toward Mr. Sanchez, and repeated the question. Mr. Sanchez swooned for a moment, then blinked rapidly, looking like he'd just woken up.

"Let me take you to Mr. Maximov's room," he said. He swept his arm to the left to show us the way.

"You kids wait outside," Doctor Nocturne ordered. "Dart, keep an eye on them."

"But . . . he's the grandson," Mr. Sanchez said, in a slight daze, pointing at me. "He has to come along or I can't take you." Reluctantly, Doctor Nocturne gestured for me to follow him and Tommy while the Dart, Teddy, and Fiona went to wait outside.

Red Malice's room was in the basement, and it stood out from the rest. A long red flag with a yellow star and hammer and sickle on it hung from the door. I recognized it as the old Soviet Union flag. The walls were covered in posters and photos and flags from a country that had ceased to exist long before I was born.

His shoes were lined up perfectly in the closet, all facing the same way, and each half an inch from the next. His suits were similarly ordered on their hangers. Everything about the room had the feel of military precision to it. The air was stale and I would have cracked a window, but since the room was in the basement, the only one was just below ceiling level.

"Be careful in here," Doctor Nocturne warned. "Tommy's brakes, the piano, the warehouse roof—there's no telling what kinds of booby traps he might have left behind."

It was far from the most encouraging pep talk I'd ever heard, but I did as I was told. I took a few cautious steps, worried that every medal, every can of borscht, even the fuzzy hat hanging on the bedpost might trigger some booby trap.

Only two things were out of place in the entire room. First, there were blueprints spread out on the table. They looked like plans for some kind of bucket on a hydraulic lift, but I couldn't tell for certain, because all the writing was in Russian. There were some photos of asteroids scattered around the table, too, so I assumed the plans were for a telescope designed to observe the meteor showers.

Tommy and Doctor Nocturne stood over the blueprints and shared a concerned glance. "What's this?" I asked.

"This is something we hoped we'd never see again," Tommy grunted.

"Let's move out," Doctor Nocturne ordered. "We need to get back to Kurtzburg."

The other thing that wasn't in its proper place was a photo album, laid open on the bed to a page with some old black-and-white photos. One photo was of a young man wearing a military uniform and one of those furry Russian caps with earflaps. In others, he was shaking hands with other Russian soldiers and military leaders. I carefully turned the page and found a photo of the same man holding Red Malice's signature weapon, the Hammersickle, a long, metal staff with a curved blade on one end and a sledgehammer on the other.

Opposite that image was a photo of him with three

black American soldiers, each wearing a patch showing a knight chess piece on his sleeve. I started to turn the page, but stopped. One of the three other soldiers had caught my eye. I leaned over to get a better look.

"Is this you?" I asked Doctor Nocturne.

He hobbled to the bed on his cane. And when I saw the chess piece head that matched the soldier's arm patch, I knew it couldn't be a coincidence.

His face remained rigid and devoid of emotion while he studied the photo in silence. Once I realized I wasn't going to get an answer to the question, I changed the subject.

"I don't get it," I said. "How does a Cold War–era Russian supervillain wind up in a run-down old folks' home in California?"

"He lost everything," Doctor Nocturne said. "He didn't have any family, because he dedicated his whole life to his country. When the Soviet Union fell apart, he couldn't go back there. Don't know how he wound up here, but it's probably because he didn't have anywhere else to go."

"Are we going?" Tommy prompted.

"Yes, we're going," Doctor Nocturne answered, turning to leave.

I tugged at his sleeve. "Do you want to take the picture?" I asked quietly.

He shook his head. "No, no reason to. The men in that picture don't exist anymore," he said.

I started to follow, but stopped in my tracks. I went back to the photo album and stared at the picture again. I picked up the album, sticking my finger into the plastic page to fish out the photo. When I lifted the book, I heard a snapping sound. I looked down and saw a closed mousetrap with some wires attached to it where the photo album had been.

That was when I heard the metal door slam loudly between me and the others. Doctor Nocturne and Tommy had made it out into the hallway, and I could hear them banging on the metal door and yelling my name. I started toward them but was interrupted by a thickly accented voice on the TV behind me.

"Ah, some of you gentlemen managed to escape the cunning traps of the Red Malice," said the gravelly voice with a heavy Russian accent. The video showed an old, white-bearded man in a red military jacket with a black star on the shoulder and a hammer and sickle on the chest. "Very good, but at long last, you shall not escape the final reckoning of Soviet Russia's finest specimen."

It seemed I had found the booby trap Doctor Nocturne had warned me about.

A Window of Opportunity

"Ammonia and chlorine," Red Malice continued on the monitor. "So simple, and so effective. Soon you will be overwhelmed by the deadly fumes of the gas produced, and no one will be able to stop me."

I charged for the door, but there was no knob or handle. It was just a thick slab of steel sealing me inside.

"There is nowhere for you to run, Dart," the TV taunted. "Torpedo, your strength cannot fight its way through that steel barrier." He leaned closer to the camera with an angry scowl. "And, Doctor Nocturne, my old nemesis, you will not be able to get inside my head; you will not be able to think your way out of this one."

From the corner of the room came a hiss as two beakers of clear liquid poured into a large bowl containing another liquid. Even from fifteen feet away, I could smell the gas within seconds. I covered my nose and mouth with my shirt, but that wouldn't do anything to filter out chlorine gas. As quickly as the chemicals started to burn in my lungs, I figured I had less than a minute to get out of the room.

"Perhaps you've noticed the window," Red Malice said teasingly. "Of course, none of you will be small enough to fit through it, but by all means, try. It might buy you an extra thirty seconds of life. Perhaps you'll be able to observe the meteor shower your NASA has been talking so much about. If you've looked around the room, you know I certainly will be watching."

The window near the ceiling was just under a foot tall and about eighteen inches wide, too small for a grown-up to squeeze through, but if I exhaled all the air in my lungs, I might be able to do it.

"I only wish I could be there in person to see you gasp your last breaths. As we face our own mortality, we look back on our lives and see that which we regret most. I am curious what you are seeing now."

There was a sink below the window. I leapt onto it while trying to hold my breath. I shoved the photo into my pocket and stretched, but even standing on top of the counter, I could barely reach the windowsill. The latch was stuck.

I looked for something to pry it open with and my eyes fell on a framed display of medals hanging on the wall to my left. Still holding my breath, I grabbed the frame and smashed it against the sink. Shards of broken glass and several heavy discs of metal attached to bright red and yellow ribbons collected in the drain.

I picked up the largest, heaviest medal—some kind of award for valor or service or honor, no doubt—and crammed it between the latch and the window frame. Leaning on it with all my weight, I managed to get the window to pop open about an inch.

That gave me enough windowsill to grab if I jumped. I slipped the medal into my pocket and leapt up, but as I hung against the wall, a startling realization came to me.

I was going to die if I couldn't do a chin-up.

One thing Coach Howard never tried during our chin-up testing was threatening my life. Something about your body's realizing that it might never again use these muscles generates more power than you can imagine. I pulled myself upward with a strength I'd never known before. I nudged the window open a bit more with my forehead and stuck my face through for the first gasp of air I'd taken since the gas had started hissing. It wasn't entirely fresh air, but the burning in my lungs and the dizziness in my head only reinforced my urgent need to escape.

Holding myself up with one arm, I braced my elbow against the outer wall of the building. Soon I had slipped through to my chest, but I couldn't find the leverage to pull myself any farther. Instead, I had to push my hands against the building and slither across the long, dead grass outside the window.

I could hear Tommy Torpedo banging against the steel barrier to the room, and from the sound of it, I guessed he might get through it in an hour or so.

"Help," I gasped. The strength in my arms was draining, and my vision had narrowed considerably. I had to get as much distance as I could between the basement and me, but with each passing second I feared the gas had already done its damage.

Just as I collapsed onto my face, my legs still hanging through the window from the knees down, I felt someone grab me by my armpits and drag me away.

At the far end of the yard, my rescuer laid me down and rolled me onto my back. The first thing I saw was

Teddy's face, inches from my own. "We've got him!" Fiona shouted back toward the building.

I coughed fitfully but couldn't fight off the inevitable. "Chlorine," I wheezed. "Ammonia. Gas."

Footsteps were approaching. "He says chlorine and ammonia," Fiona repeated.

I fought to keep my eyes open, but it proved to be a losing battle.

"Stay with me here, Nate," Teddy pleaded. "Don't close your eyes, buddy."

All I could think at that moment was that at least I'd gotten out of the basement. At least I wouldn't die alone.

And then came the darkness. Restful, eternal darkness.

o o o

For a dead guy, I felt a lot of pain in my chest. I guess I was expecting more everlasting peace than sharp blows to the sternum.

"Stop it!" a voice warned from above. "You're going to break his ribs."

"I have to keep his heart beating until the paramedics get here," another disembodied voice—which sounded a lot like Teddy's—replied.

"His heart is fine," said another voice. It sounded

remarkably like Doctor Nocturne's. "And he's breathing, too, so you can knock off the mouth-to-mouth. Just stick this under his nose."

Suddenly, I felt a jolt as though I had been punched in the nose, and my eyes shot open. I swatted a hand I later realized was Fiona's away from my face, sending a small packet of smelling salts flying into the tall, dead grass that surrounded me. The first thing I came to focus on was Teddy looming above me, preparing to give me CPR, his hands positioned over the center of my chest and his elbows locked.

"Wha—what happened?" I gasped. "I was dead and—"

"You weren't dead," Doctor Nocturne barked. "That wasn't chlorine gas. It was knockout gas. You took a nap for five minutes, so stop being so dramatic."

"Red Malice," I whispered hoarsely as I sat up. "I saw him. There was a video. He set the trap to catch whichever of you survived his earlier attempts on your lives."

"What else did Red Malice say?" Doctor Nocturne asked.

I was still groggy. "He said none of you could escape, because the window was too small, but maybe you could see the . . . um . . ." I tried to replay the video in my head.

"The meteor shower. Oh, because that's what he was doing. Watching the meteor shower. It didn't make much sense."

Doctor Nocturne, the Dart, and Tommy Torpedo looked nervously at one another. Maybe it didn't make sense to me, but it seemed to have meaning to them.

"We need to get back to Kurtzburg," Doctor Nocturne insisted. "Dart, you go ahead. It's going to take us about fifteen minutes to get to the graveyard and use the zombie's crypt."

"Actually," Fiona started, then looked at me to make sure it was okay. I nodded. "Right after you left, Captain Zombie remembered there was a closer cemetery."

We hurried across the street to the mausoleum, but I held Teddy and Fiona back. There was something that had been bothering me.

"While I was knocked out, I thought I heard..." I looked intently at Teddy. "Did Doctor Nocturne say 'mouth-to-mouth'?"

Americans Love the Apple Pie

Captain Zombie was nowhere to be found, so we waited, some of us more patiently than others. While Tommy Torpedo nervously drummed his fingers on the marble bar, Doctor Nocturne paced furiously, the Dart adjusted the oxygen tube going to his nose, and I wiped my lips for the three dozenth time.

"I thought you were dead, Nate," Teddy confided. "I had to do something."

"Next time you think I'm dead, you have my permission to do nothing. I appreciate that you were trying to help, but let's never speak of this again."

"Nate and Teddy sitting in a tree," Fiona sang without moving her lips, looking around curiously and shrugging as if she didn't know who was doing it. "K-I-S-S-I-N-G."

"Get it out of your system while we're here," I grumbled. "Once we're home, this never happened."

"Speaking of home, it's about eight o'clock back in Kanigher Falls," Fiona informed us. "We may want to start wrapping this up to make sure we're home in time for the meteor shower."

"Who cares about the meteor shower?" I groaned, still fighting off the effects of the gas.

"Well, to be honest, I'm more concerned about making it home in time to not get grounded for the remainder of winter break," Fiona admitted.

She was right. Besides, Doctor Nocturne hadn't wanted me tagging along in the first place, much less two more kids. Red Malice's trap had failed, just like his earlier ones, so it seemed to make sense to call it a night.

"Why now?" Tommy asked aloud.

"What are you talking about?" Doctor Nocturne replied gruffly.

"None of us has heard anything from Red Malice in decades," he said, elaborating. "The guy hasn't gotten a parking ticket in twenty years. What would make him decide to attempt three murders this week?"

"Boredom?" Teddy suggested. "Did you see that place? I don't think they even had basic cable. Same thing every single day; nothing ever changes—"

"Well, something changed," Fiona chimed in. "Remember what that Sanchez guy told us? Doctors found out he was going to die of cancer."

I could see the mixed emotions on the former superheroes' faces. Even I felt a little sad hearing the news that Red Malice was going to die. Then I had a sudden thought about the end of his video.

"What would Red Malice's biggest regret in life be?" I posed the question to the entire group. "In the video, that was part of the booby trap. He said, 'As we face our own mortality, we look back on our lives and see that which we regret most.'"

"Getting his butt handed to him by us," Tommy Torpedo laughed.

"Never cornering the apple market," the Dart suggested. "Remember when he posed as a rich investor—hhheeeehhh—and bought up all those apple farms, then made them stop shipping apples?"

"Why did he do that?" Fiona asked.

"'Americans love the apple pie!'" the Dart mimicked in a bad Russian accent before another coughing fit.

"'Without their precious apples, they will crack—hheeeehh—and glorious Soviet Union will prevail.'"

Doctor Nocturne was noticeably silent. "What do you think, Doctor Nocturne?" I asked.

"I *think* it doesn't really matter, Nate. I *think* I've had enough of playing superhero with you, and I *think* I need to get back to Kurtzburg, which is why I *think* Captain Zombie better get back here soon."

"But he's not here yet," Fiona said challengingly. "So why don't you tell us what you know? This guy just tried to kill Nate, so I *think* you're wrong. It does matter."

The Dart chuckled quietly while Doctor Nocturne stared down the twelve-year-old girl who dared to defy him. "I like her," the Dart stated. "She's spunky."

"Red Malice was a zealot," Doctor Nocturne said. "He believed in the Soviet Union and communism, and he hated America. He was always plotting to destroy capitalism. I guess if he has one regret, it's probably that he was never able to do that."

"That's kind of what I was afraid of," I said. "I think . . . " I began, pulling the pieces together, considering what President McKinley had told me. "I think Red Malice is going to try to destroy America for the glory of the Soviet Union before he dies."

Even my own friends weren't sure what to make of my theory.

"You do realize there hasn't been a Soviet Union in more than twenty years, right?" Fiona asked.

"All the more reason to strike this blow before he dies," I suggested. "This guy who used to be a supervillain lost his country, got old, and now he's been told he's going to die. He's powerless. And nobody likes that feeling."

The three elderly men looked uncomfortable.

"It's like President McKinley said," I continued.

"How did President McKinley know about Red Malice?" Teddy asked. Fiona silenced him with an elbow to the ribs. "Ow!"

"If his biggest regret is that he never overcame Doctor Nocturne, Tommy Torpedo, or the Dart and struck a blow for his motherland, I think that's exactly what he intends to do before he dies," I explained. "We just need to figure out what he's going to do. That's why I've been trying to think about what he said in that video."

Doctor Nocturne looked reluctantly at Tommy Torpedo, who nodded like we'd gotten the same answers on our math homework.

"Fifty years ago, Red Malice attacked Kurtzburg," Tommy Torpedo said. "All three of us were there. We're pretty sure after what we saw and what Nate heard him say on the video that he's going to try it again."

The conversation was interrupted by Captain Zombie's return. He was wearing his orange and yellow superhero costume and had obviously just been on patrol around his hometown of Haney. He seemed surprised to find so many guests waiting for him at the mausoleum.

"Oh, a full house tonight," he said. "Let me change out of this old thing and—Fiona, could you go through the board games and find one we can play with seven people? Pictionary's good, but the teams will be uneven. Then again, Teddy can't draw anything more complicated than a hot dog, so it probably balances out—"

"We need to get back to Kurtzburg, Zombie," Doctor Nocturne demanded.

"That's a great idea. I hear the meteor shower is beautiful on the East Coast right now," Captain Zombie said. "Like nature's fireworks."

"We don't have time for this, Zombie," Doctor Nocturne insisted. "There's a dangerous supervillain on the loose."

"Besides, I can draw lots of things," Teddy argued in his defense. "You're just a terrible guesser. That's why we lost last time."

"Zombie!" Doctor Nocturne shouted impatiently. "Kurtzburg. *Now.*"

Captain Zombie's scaly forehead wrinkled slightly, though you'd only have noticed if you'd spent a lot of time around him. Dead flesh isn't very expressive. The mausoleum seemed to tremble a bit. "Excuse me," Captain Zombie said in a deeper voice than we were accustomed to hearing from him. It came from deep in his chest but crackled with power to rival death itself. "I am not running a taxi service. I am more than happy to help you get to Kurtzburg, but the least you can do in my home is show me the courtesy of *asking* me instead of telling me."

The tomb quaked with his words, and I questioned all the times my friends and I had joked about the Power of the Graveyard without really understanding it.

"Zomb . . . *Captain* Zombie," Doctor Nocturne began.

I jumped in. "Would you please help us get to Kurtzburg, Captain Zombie? Doc Noc and his friends think a supervillain might be up to something, and we need to check it out."

Captain Zombie smiled as best he could with lips that had largely rotted away. "I would be happy to, Nate. Just one thing first." He turned to Teddy. "You drew a house and then you circled the door frame and just kept circling for a full minute. How is that 'return address'? Don't tell me I'm a bad guesser."

We all walked up the stairs to the exit, where Doctor Nocturne had stashed his motorcycle. The Dart couldn't make it up with his walker, so he leaned on Fiona's arm for support while I carried it for him.

Teddy pulled up the rear, mumbling to himself, imitating Captain Zombie. "'Is it a house? It's a house. How about house? I'm guessing house. If it's a house, then we win.'"

"I'm going to join you, if you don't mind," Captain Zombie said while Doctor Nocturne and Tommy Torpedo mounted the motorcycle and climbed into the sidecar. "I really want to check out this meteor shower."

He pulled open the door, and we stepped out beneath the Kurtzburg sky, which was striped with falling stars. The sight left us all gasping at the beauty of it, and I looked forward to getting back home to watch it again later.

But the beauty part only lasted about five seconds. Then Captain Zombie's stomach exploded into my hands.

Is That a Meteor or a Meteorite?

It took me a second to realize that the dust I was inhaling was from Captain Zombie's shattered bones and dry, dead skin. "What was that?" he shouted as he stared down at the hole in his belly. It was as big around as a two-liter bottle of soda. He glanced back at me and grabbed the handful of intestines from my loose grasp.

He stuffed his guts back in with one hand and drew out a small smoking rock with the other.

"It that a meteor?" Teddy wondered.

"Technically, I think it's a meteorite," Captain Zombie said, correcting him. "Once a meteor hits something, it becomes a meteorite. Or is it the other way around?"

We heard a faint whistling from the sky, and there

was a small explosion just to the left of the mausoleum entrance. "Another one?" Fiona asked. "What are the odds of that?"

"Better than you think," Tommy Torpedo responded, pointing to the sky. A hail of meteors, their long glowing tails behind them, was screaming toward us.

Tommy Torpedo leapt from the sidecar, or at least attempted to leap from it. It might be more accurate to say he heaved himself from the sidecar, nearly tumbling face-first onto the ground. Without a second of hesitation, he put himself between the meteors and Teddy. A meteor struck his sizable belly, knocking him backward onto my friend, but otherwise leaving them both unharmed.

Captain Zombie planted his feet and thrust his hands forward, commanding the graveyard to protect us. Trees leaned their branches in front of us to shield us from the hail of rocks. The ground rose, creating a berm capped by a line of headstones for extra protection.

A large meteor tore through the trees' canopy and whistled toward Fiona and me, leaving a path of burning leaves in its wake. Its white-hot surface glowed with a blinding intensity, and I couldn't help wondering if I would burn to death or be smashed to a pulp first.

Then it occurred to me that I shouldn't have had time

to examine the situation so closely. It would have taken only a second for the meteor to zip from the tree line through my chest, yet it had seemed to stop, frozen in time. And then I felt something bump into the small of my back.

Fiona and I both turned. The Dart's walker was nudging us forward at what would have appeared to be superspeed to anyone watching. For us, it just looked like the rest of the world had slowed to a crawl. The smoke from the burning surface of the meteor billowed behind it so slowly it appeared to be a long strand of white cotton candy. The embers from the burning trees floated in the air, suspended between gravity's pull and heat's rise. In the distance, the Kurtzburg skyline was under similar attack. There were hundreds — maybe thousands — of meteors streaming down on the city.

As the Dart pushed us gently toward safety, wheezing on his oxygen tank, I glanced back to see how the others were faring. Tommy Torpedo's mouth hung open in the middle of a defiant scream; his arm was cocked back to punch an incoming meteor. Unfortunately, while he might have had the strength of one hundred men, they were one hundred eighty-two-year-old men. I watched in sickening slow motion as he mistimed the punch, took the meteor squarely in the jaw, and was flung backward, head over heels.

Doctor Nocturne twisted the motorcycle's handlebars to get it behind the mausoleum for some extra cover. A small meteor, no larger than a golf ball, was on course to hit him squarely in the back of his skull, but a pair of decaying hands reached up from beneath the ground and grabbed his pant leg, dragging him off the motorcycle and onto the ground. The small meteor skimmed his head by a few inches before cracking a granite tombstone ten feet away.

The large meteor headed for Fiona, the Dart, and me floated just feet away, and I felt a wave of heat.

"Keep moving," the Dart wheezed.

Another, smaller meteor came streaking toward us, but the Dart didn't see it, because he was concentrating on Fiona and me.

"Look out!" I shouted, pointing at the glowing white rock. But there was nothing he could do without abandoning us.

For a moment, I felt guilty about shoving an old man to the ground, especially one as frail as the Dart. But given the alternative, I didn't have much choice. I grabbed his shoulders and pulled him down, out of the path of the meteor.

As soon as we hit the ground, everything returned to normal speed, just in time for me to see the Dart's walker destroyed by the impact of the meteor. It had shattered the hinge that held the left side of the contraption together.

"Anybody hurt?" Doctor Nocturne shouted.

"A little help?" called Tommy Torpedo, who was lying on his back, rocking back and forth, unable to get up. Teddy tried to pull him to his feet, but looked more likely to topple over than to help Tommy.

"I'm going to help Teddy," I told Fiona. "You help the Dart."

"No," the Dart protested. "Don't bother with me." He took a deep, raspy breath. "I think I just broke my hip. Besides, without my walker, I'm useless."

"You still have your superspeed," Fiona said, encouraging him.

"What good is speed without legs?" He took off the ring and stared at it in his palm, looking sad and frustrated.

"See if you can get the Dart back into the mausoleum," I told Fiona. "That's probably the safest place right now."

I got my legs under me and tried to run to Tommy

Torpedo while staying as low to the ground as possible. Teddy and I each took a hand and pulled, getting him back to his feet. It was only once he was up that we saw the gruesome gaggle of zombie hands that had emerged from the graveyard's floor to help push Tommy up.

"Thanks," I said to the disembodied arms. One corpse lifted his head above the surface and replied with a thumbs-up.

Using Tommy as a shield, I made my way to the back of the mausoleum. Doctor Nocturne had mounted the motorcycle and was waiting for the big man to get into the sidecar.

"We need to go back inside until this passes," I told him.

"This isn't going to pass, Nate," he replied. "Red Malice is behind this. And it's just the beginning."

"How do you know?" I asked. "This meteor shower comes along every fifty years. We talked about it in science class."

"Because we've seen it before," Tommy bellowed. "It's what I was talking about down in the tomb. Fifty years ago, Red Malice aimed a tractor beam at a passing meteor shower. His plan was to pull the largest asteroid to Earth and crash it into Kurtzburg."

"The blueprints," I muttered, recalling the photos of asteroids on the table.

"We thought we had destroyed it," Tommy continued. "Either he salvaged it or rebuilt it, but either way, he's trying to bring one of those asteroids up there down on Kurtzburg."

"That would kill everyone in the city," Teddy said.

"Not just the city," Doctor Nocturne said, correcting him. "That's how the dinosaurs died. Red Malice's plan was to destroy the entire East Coast and much of the Midwest. A large enough impact would cause tidal waves, earthquakes, and dust storms that would block out the sun for weeks. Millions of people would die."

"We have to stop him," Teddy said.

"You don't have to do anything," Doctor Nocturne snapped. "Get back in that crypt, where it's safe. Tell the Dart to meet us—"

"The Dart's walker is broken," I informed them. "He's not going anywhere."

Tommy Torpedo and Doctor Nocturne shared a concerned glance and looked over to see Fiona dragging their friend to safety.

"Maybe we should get Steph—the other Doctor Nocturne to help," I suggested.

"No time to track her down," her father argued. "Besides, she already has plenty to take care of if these meteors are hitting all over Kurtzburg."

"Then at least take Captain Zombie with you," Teddy pleaded.

"No good," I replied. "Once he gets a couple blocks away from the cemetery, he'll lose his powers."

While Tommy hefted his leg over the sidecar and squeezed himself into the seat, I pulled Teddy aside.

"Fiona's going to need help with the Dart," I said. "I'm pretty sure there has to be a medical supply store near a cemetery somewhere in the world."

"Good thinking," he agreed. "Let's go."

I shook my head. "No, it's up to you." I turned and pulled up the hood on my sweatshirt. With a few running steps, I jumped onto the back of the sidecar and landed on the seat of the motorcycle behind Doctor Nocturne.

"Where do you think you're going?" Doctor Nocturne barked.

I fished the mask from my pocket and slipped it over my eyes. "You're supposed to be training me," I reminded him.

Sidekicks Went Out of Style in the Eighties

It wasn't hard to locate Red Malice. His machine pulsed a bright red beam of light into the sky that not only pulled down a rain of meteors but also served as a huge neon sign that might as well have read EVIL SUPERVILLAIN AT WORK! We followed a coastal road toward the beam of light and ended up in a clearing that overlooked the city.

Once we rounded the final turn in the road, we came upon a machine the size of a house. Its base was wide and flat, with a large metal housing on one end. A hydraulic arm with four or five hinges rose from the base, making the machine jut up toward the sky in a giant zigzag. A large rounded piece of machinery that looked like the barrel of a laser cannon was attached at the end of the arm, thanks to a mess of wires and tubing. A beam of red light projected from the end of the laser cannon, brightening the night sky like an enormous searchlight.

An old man was standing on the deck of the tractor beam. He was stooped over and hobbled a bit, but he was still robust enough to look dangerous. He wore a furry black hat with earflaps folded up on the sides and a red military uniform. His closely trimmed white beard framed his wicked smile perfectly, and he leaned casually on a long yellow staff that crackled with energy. On one end was a large sledgehammer, and on the other was a razor-sharp sickle. The Hammersickle.

"I am so happy you chose to face me in person," Red Malice shouted over the crackle of the cannon. "At first I thought, *Yuri, don't be a fool. Doctor Nocturne is not stupid. He would not be so predictable.* Then I thought, *No, he is stupid* and *predictable.*"

Doctor Nocturne dismounted the motorcycle, never taking his eyes off his old enemy. Tommy, on the other hand, needed a little help getting free of the sidecar.

"What's the matter, old friends?" Red Malice called. "Shall we catch up on old times? I hear that your car insurance rates will be going up, Tommy! And, Doctor Nocturne, word is that you recently had a bad fall off the roof of a warehouse in your beloved Kurtzburg. Is that why you use the cane now? Your healing abilities not up to snuff any longer?"

"You should know it takes more than a tumble to stop me," Doctor Nocturne retorted.

"Come, come, my friends. Gather around!"

He swung the hammer end of his weapon up into a charging Tommy Torpedo. Bulletproof skin was one thing, but Tommy's chin was no match for the Hammersickle. Red Malice's signature weapon offered two lethal options. The hammer hit with the impact of a wrecking ball, even in the hands of an elderly man. The sickle was capable of slicing through a reinforced beam of hardened steel as easily as it would a marshmallow.

Tommy flew into the air, clearing my head by at least ten feet. He sailed backward in a long arc and landed at the base of a tree about thirty feet away. The tree trunk cracked from the impact.

"Oh, Tommy!" Red Malice cackled. "If you wanted a closer look at what I am doing, you should have just asked." He walked to a control panel on the housing of the mechanical arm. "I have waited so many years for this night. This meteor shower is only the beginning. Most of these tiny sparks in the sky, these pebbles falling around us, are just debris from the surface of Asteroid D-1974. The asteroid itself is large enough to crush your beloved city. And nearby, in your nation's capital, the White House and your Congress will be gone in a cloud of dust. At long last, capitalism will be crushed and the glorious Soviet Union shall rise again! For once, you cannot stop me!"

As Tommy shook his head and rubbed his jaw, Red Malice jabbed the sickle threateningly toward him. Tommy rolled onto his side and braced himself against the broken tree trunk to get back to his feet. He charged again and Red Malice smiled wickedly, spinning the Hammersickle with ease and burying the hammer in Tommy's considerable belly.

Tommy's invulnerability would let him take blow after blow from the hammer, but I doubted he'd withstand the sickle. We had to help him.

Doctor Nocturne ambled toward his nemesis, leaning heavily on his cane. I suspected being pulled off the motorcycle earlier might have done more damage to his bad hip than he was letting on. I rushed to his side.

"What is this, Doctor? You have a sidekick?" Red Malice taunted. "I thought those went out of style in the eighties."

"Technically, I prefer to be called a 'trusted advisor'!" I shouted back.

We needed to shut down the tractor beam. Small meteors were landing in the trees all around us, and if Tommy and Doctor Nocturne were right, it wouldn't be long before one of their big brothers was on its way.

"Can you distract him?" I asked.

"I've been distracting him for fifty years," Doctor Nocturne said.

"I'm going to get to that control panel and shut it down before it does any more damage."

I charged toward the tractor beam's base. Red Malice smiled viciously and clutched the Hammersickle with both hands. As I neared him, he spun to look behind him, allowing me to slip past and get to the platform.

"Your old telepathic tricks," Red Malice said, laughing, to Doctor Nocturne while tapping his temple. "It's been so long I almost missed them."

"Yeah, did you miss this, too?" Doctor Nocturne whirled him around and landed a punch squarely on the old Russian's jaw. "Because that's one of my favorites."

The control panel was difficult to comprehend. I pulled out the keyboard and hit a button. The old computer monitor was barely readable, with the distorted image rolling from side to side. It took me a moment to figure out that the screen that popped up was asking for a password.

I hit enter but got a red screen. I couldn't make out any of the words, because the white and red pixels bled together into a pink mess. Regardless, I understood "Access Denied." I wasn't going to be able to do anything without the password.

Doctor Nocturne held back the Hammersickle with his cane, baring his teeth at the Soviet supervillain. I watched the two old men struggling as I tried to figure out the password—and then a thought came to me. "Old men," I whispered to myself.

I typed P-A-S-S-W-O-R-D.

Whatever the blinking screen said, I assumed it was something like "Access Granted." Hope welled up in my chest for a moment as I waited for the next screen to load so I could shut down the beam and save the day.

A small radar screen flickered to life to the right of the monitor. The screen looked like someone had spilled salt on it, and I quickly concluded that each of the tiny white dots was a meteor within the range of the beam. To the left of center were two larger spots, which had to be the giant asteroids Moonrock had been warning about in his blog post.

Unfortunately, since I couldn't read anything on the computer monitor, I had no choice but to peck at the keyboard and watch the monitor switch screens, seemingly at random. The barrel of the tractor beam shifted in several directions as I punched different keys, but while every key seemed to do something, none of them was stopping the beam. With each attempt, the radar screen shifted as well. I determined that the center must represent the focus of the tractor beam.

It didn't seem likely I was going to be able to shut down the tractor beam on random chance alone, and every keystroke also ran the risk of making things worse. What if I intensified the beam's strength or steered it directly toward the asteroids? There had to be another way to stop it.

I gazed upward for some kind of divine inspiration. And there it was, directly above me: the barrel of the machinery, firing its bright red beam into space. If I couldn't shut it down, I would have to try to break it.

Best Friends, Like It or Not

While Doctor Nocturne parried a blow from the Hammersickle with his cane, I pulled myself onto the narrow, rounded housing for the tractor beam's hydraulic arm. It was thin, but it was wider than a stalagmite, so my training seemed to have finally paid off. I found my equilibrium easily and leapt to the first hinge in the arm, balancing on a ball joint that was smaller than a soccer ball. I reached up and grabbed the top of the zigzag, pulling myself to the highest point of the machine.

The power emanating from the barrel of the tractor beam shook the entire arm, making balancing on the joint that connected the two difficult. Compared to spending an entire evening standing on a stalagmite, though, it was like a relaxing day on the beach.

The barrel had several access panels around it, but

they were labeled in Russian. I pulled one open, bracing myself against the cannon. Inside were more wires than I could ever hope to count, some circuit boards, and a crystal. *When in doubt,* I told myself, *smash.* But I had neglected to bring a tool fit for the task.

I looked around desperately. Below me, Doctor Nocturne continued to fight valiantly, but I knew his hip would give out soon.

"Get down from there!" Red Malice shouted, pointing at me with his sickle. I could hear the crackling of its yellow tip near my feet. "That is very dangerous, little boy. Now, come down. You do not know what you are doing up there and you are going to get hurt."

At once, he was tackled from behind by Tommy Torpedo. They both flew forward, the Hammersickle slicing through a large part of the eight-inch-thick hinge that held the barrel of the tractor beam to the arm. Red Malice rolled with the tackle and sprang to his feet with surprising agility for such an old guy. The blade of the sickle was near Tommy's throat.

Red Malice laughed forcefully, spun the Hammersickle, and dropped the hammer end onto Tommy's face.

In desperation, I patted my pockets, looking for something to save the day. Maybe I could pry the crystal out with my house key or —

Suddenly, I became aware of the weight in my pocket. I reached in and drew out the dull copper medal with Russian letters on it. Without a second thought, I gripped it by the edge and smashed it into the tractor beam crystal.

The entire contraption shuddered and my feet slipped from my perch, but I managed to grab the arm of the beam to stop my fall.

While he fought Doctor Nocturne, Red Malice had his back to me, exposing a huge hammer-and-sickle logo on his back. In that moment, it looked like a bull's-eye to me. With all my strength, I swung from the tractor beam and launched myself feetfirst into his back. He stumbled forward and fell off the edge of the platform.

Something had been bothering me during the battle, and now I had a few seconds to talk to Doctor Nocturne. Something was fishy about Red Malice's plan.

"I don't think this is what we think it is," I yelled.

"You've seen this thing in action, Nate," he replied. "It's a tractor beam."

"No, I mean Red Malice's plan to destroy you and

Western civilization at the same time. I don't think that's really his intention. I was wrong."

President McKinley had been right, but I'd drawn the wrong conclusion from his words. As death grew closer for Red Malice, he had clung to his greatest desires and beliefs. But destroying America wasn't Red Malice's greatest desire. And failing to do so wasn't his biggest regret.

For two nights, I'd thought I was watching three old men trying to relive their glory days, but really it had been four old men. Red Malice's greatest desire was to go out with a bang. He hadn't wanted to spend his last days wasting away alone in an old folks' home.

"He tried to kill us, Nate," Doctor Nocturne argued.

"I don't think he did," I suggested. "He knows all of your powers and abilities. If he really wanted to kill Tommy Torpedo, why do it with a car accident that Tommy would easily survive? The Dart dodged that piano because of his superspeed. And you wouldn't have died from a fall through a warehouse skylight. Red Malice knew that. If he was trying to kill you guys, he picked the worst ways to do it in every case."

Doctor Nocturne thought for a moment.

"Even the trap in the old folks' home wasn't deadly," I said. "He used knockout gas. He wasn't trying to kill anyone. Did you notice he keeps hitting Tommy with the hammer end of that thing? If he wanted to kill him, he could slice him in half with the sickle. And he hasn't hit you with it yet."

The menacing tractor beam continued to whir like a million blenders as circuits popped, wires burned up, and resistors overloaded, drawing Doctor Nocturne's attention. But before he could ask a question, I answered it for him.

"When I turned on the tractor beam's radar screen, the beam wasn't aimed at the big asteroids," I recalled. "They're heading west and the beam was aimed to the east. There was no way the beam would ever lock on to them."

"He still rained meteors down on all of us in the cemetery."

"Yeah, but those were no real threat to you or Tommy or even the Dart — if he hadn't been busy rescuing Fiona and me. And, sure, one of us could have been hurt, but how was he to know three kids would be tagging along? Remember? Sidekicks went out of style in the eighties."

"But why?" Doctor Nocturne asked softly. He seemed to be seriously considering my theory.

"Because he's dying," I answered. "And he doesn't want to do it alone in a hospital bed. He wants to go out doing what he loves, surrounded by people who care about him. You said it yourself: He has no family, and his home vanished twenty years ago." I shrugged and broke the next news gently. "Like it or not, I think you guys are his best friends."

On the ground, Red Malice tangled with a temporarily conscious Tommy Torpedo, swinging the Hammersickle into Tommy's gut and hurling him end over end into the branches of a leafless cherry blossom tree.

"Friends, huh?" Doctor Nocturne grunted.

Red Malice jumped back onto the deck with us, spinning the Hammersickle menacingly. "One more round, Doctor," he said. "I think we have time for that before my tractor beam makes contact with the asteroid that will be your undoing."

Doctor Nocturne pushed me away, staggered on his bad hip, and raised his fists. Red Malice swung the Hammersickle high above his head and brought it down with both hands on Doctor Nocturne. However, in his wide sweeping arc, he nicked the bottom of the tractor beam barrel. That might not have been a big deal had the Hammersickle not been so powerful, and had the joint holding the barrel to the arm not already been partially severed.

The tiny ding was all it took to twist the metal, sending the malfunctioning tractor beam crashing to the deck. I instinctively leaned back, but there was no way I would escape the metal piece, until it suddenly slowed down considerably.

The barrel of the tractor beam twisted and pointed almost straight down, tearing up the deck rivet by rivet. The metal at the end of the arm was wound like a washcloth someone had wrung out. Red Malice stared upward in surprise as he pushed Doctor Nocturne out of the way and off the platform to safety. Meanwhile, I was being dragged away while the beam flickered and died, the wires connecting it to its power source snapping as it fell in slow motion onto the spot where I had just been standing.

I heaved a sigh of relief and turned to thank the Dart for rescuing me, but when I craned my neck to look behind me, I saw Fiona.

"Fiona? How did you—?"

Once we were safely away from the tractor beam, she

stopped and waved the fingers of her left hand, showing me the Dart's blue metal ring. Almost immediately, she staggered and fell to one knee.

"Whoa, he told me it would tire me out, but . . ." She yanked the ring from her finger and flung it to the ground, falling forward onto both hands and heaving like she might throw up.

I reached for the ring.

"Don't touch it with your hand!" she shouted before she collapsed facedown.

"Fiona!" I grabbed her by the shoulders and rolled her over. I knew enough from my mom to check for vital signs. She was breathing and her pulse was strong but racing.

Then she started to snore. She wasn't dying—she was just exhausted.

With the tractor beam disabled, the meteor strikes had stopped. Sure she was safe, I left Fiona to rush back toward the crash. Doctor Nocturne struggled to get up from the ground, leaning on the tractor beam's deck for support until he could find his cane. Tommy emerged from the nearby trees, unharmed.

Red Malice, on the other hand, hadn't been so lucky.

I heard him groan from beneath the shattered remains

of the tractor beam's cannon. Tommy Torpedo hurried to lift the several tons of metal, glass, and electronics off him. "The good guys come through again," Red Malice said softly. "Thank you, my friends, for humoring a dying old man. Please, when you think of me, think not of an enemy."

"Friend, enemy — when you get to be our age, Yuri, you know nothing's that simple," Doctor Nocturne assured him.

"I am happy you did not get hurt falling off the roof," Red Malice moaned weakly.

"I didn't fall off the roof," Doctor Nocturne told him. "My daughter was the one on patrol. I've . . . retired and . . . she's Doctor Nocturne now."

Red Malice's eyes opened wide with regret. "Your daughter? I had no idea. Is she okay?"

"Yeah," Doctor Nocturne said softly with a chuckle. "She's tough."

"Like her father," Red Malice added. He coughed and blood flecked his lips. "I will see you . . . wherever it is old soldiers like us wind up." He closed his eyes and his body went limp.

"*Da svidaniya*, old friend," Doctor Nocturne whispered.

The Next Generation

Doctor Nocturne and Tommy stayed in Kurtzburg to deal with the authorities. Somehow Captain Zombie managed to get me, Teddy, and Fiona home in time for the meteor shower. I called my dad, and he met us at the park to watch with us. Some amateur astronomers had set up their telescopes and we took turns watching.

"Would you look at that?" Dad gasped. "They're so close it feels like they're coming down on top of you."

Teddy and I shared a knowing glance. Fiona probably would have done the same if she hadn't fallen asleep at a nearby picnic table.

After the meteor shower, Dad managed to fit all our bikes in the back of his car. Then he dropped off Teddy and Fiona at their houses.

The next morning, I woke to the smell of chocolate

chip pancakes and went downstairs to find my dad standing at the counter, watching TV.

"Tough blow for the Rhinos," a sportscaster announced. "Looks like fan favorite Bullethead Johnson is going in for knee surgery . . . again. He'll miss the team's final game of the season on Sunday. Johnson's not talking about retirement just yet, but it's hard to imagine a lot of teams falling all over themselves to pick up a forty-year-old with bad knees next season."

"Sorry, Dad," I said.

Dad turned in surprise. "What are you doing up? I didn't think you woke up before noon during vacation."

"I smelled pancakes," I said sleepily. "Sorry about Bullethead."

"No reason to be," he assured me as he poured pancake batter onto the griddle. "The Rhinos have a real talent in Sheffield. It's time for the next generation to shine." He sprinkled a handful of chocolate chips into the pancakes. "You planning to go work out with Teddy again?"

"Um, yeah," I replied. "I think so."

"How's that going?" he asked. "Seeing any progress?"

I thought back on the previous night and nodded. "Yeah, I think so. I did a chin-up."

After Dad left for work, Teddy and Fiona came over

to help go through my comic books and find images for Ultraviolet's hidden base while we watched Fiona's *Nightowl* DVD. She also brought along some issues of *Sisteroid*, which she claimed might help give the headquarters a more feminine touch.

"And that is why nobody reads *Sisteroid*," Teddy argued.

Later, when I arrived in Doctor Nocturne's cavernous headquarters, I finally learned what Stephanie and Phantom Ranger meant about the tennis balls.

"Watch out," Doctor Nocturne shouted as another ball whizzed past my ear. I jerked my head out of the way, which threw off my balance and made me slip off the stalagmite onto the mats.

"This is crazy," I protested. "There's no way I can keep my balance and dodge those things at the same time."

"Oh, you dodged four of them before you fell off that last time," Doctor Nocturne pointed out. "That's pretty good for your first night. Now, jump back up there."

I climbed up onto the stalagmite again, found my balance, and prepared for the next bombardment.

"Every time I hit you with one of these, you owe me twenty-five push-ups," he reminded me. The first tennis ball came right at my knees. Without thinking, I leapt about six inches off the stalagmite, just high enough for the ball to pass under my feet, and landed firmly back in place. I'm not sure which of us was more shocked by the move.

"Nicely done!" Doctor Nocturne cheered. I wasn't sure what to make of his praise, but if I could get used to the yelling, I didn't think it would be too difficult to get used to the encouragement.

I was so stunned by the move myself that I didn't see the next ball coming until it hit me squarely in the chest. I toppled and landed on the mats, immediately rolling over to execute twenty-five push-ups.

When I finished, Doctor Nocturne offered me a hand. "That's probably enough for tonight," he said.

"What? But it hasn't even been an hour yet."

He shrugged. "You've had a couple of busy evenings. We can take it easy tonight. Besides, I have some business to take care of." He walked over to his motorcycle and tossed me the spare helmet.

"Aren't you going to change?" I asked, pointing to the wardrobe. Seeing him in anything but the full blue suit and cape outside of the cave was unheard of.

He shook his head. "I got to thinking about what I told Red Malice," he explained. "I'm retired. My daughter is

Doctor Nocturne now. And it's not fair for me to try to take that from her or share it with her. When my time to go comes, I don't want to be like Red Malice, with nothing to cling to but what I used to be and how I used to feel. It's time for me to use my strengths elsewhere. Like in training you, building secret lairs, stuff like that. Speaking of which . . ."

A brief motorcycle ride from Kurtzburg to Kanigher Falls via Captain Zombie's crypt later, we were standing outside the newly constructed Ditko Middle School. A door was propped open.

We went inside, walking the hallway where only some of the tile was laid. Pallets of sinks and toilets were stationed outside the bathrooms, waiting to be installed. Wires hung from holes in the ceilings, awaiting the fluorescent fixtures that would eventually light our halls.

Ultraviolet waited for us, her purple and white goggles perched atop her head. She was examining a classroom that would be hers in a matter of weeks.

"I have a stack of comics full of secret headquarters stuff for you," I told her. "If you want to swing by my house later, I can give them to you."

"Thanks, Nate," she said. "I'll be sure to look those over."

"Can you please be gentle with them?" I pleaded.

"I'll do my best," she promised. "Now, on the subject of secret lairs . . ."

Doctor Nocturne nodded and led us to a janitor's closet. He stepped into the closet and gestured to the floor drain in the middle of a shallow basin, where the janitor would empty his mop bucket. "What do you think?"

Ultraviolet and I stared at the drain, and then at each other. Doctor Nocturne sighed.

"Nate, get in the basin."

"What?"

"Just stand on the drain."

I stepped in and Doctor Nocturne turned the faucet on. With a shudder, the floor beneath me began to sink.

"What is this supposed to do exact—" My question was lost when the floor dropped sharply and I plummeted through the darkness of a round abyss. By the time I opened my mouth to scream, I'd already reached the bottom.

Though I'd safely touched down, I was in complete darkness. Carefully, I put my arms out in front of me and groped at the round walls of the shaft where I stood. Finally, I found a hole in the wall and reached out into the emptiness before me. With my right foot, I tapped around to be certain there was a floor ahead and not a sharp drop into nothingness.

Reassured, I stepped off the round platform. The moment I did, I sensed it rising slowly behind me before it shot back to the top of the shaft. My stepping out of the shaft also triggered a few motion-activated lights, which slowly flickered to life. They were dim, but I could see that I was inside a large cavern.

Several crates were stacked to my left, all of them far too large to have fit down the single-person elevator platform I'd just ridden. The floor had been leveled with concrete, but the walls and ceiling were still natural bedrock. Among the crates I found computers, lab equipment, and a plasma monitor bigger than a school bus.

"Nate?" I heard Ultraviolet call from the elevator, which hadn't made a sound bringing her down.

"I'm over here by the crates," I shouted back.

I was happy to see a look of bewilderment on her face. "I take it you hadn't seen this yet, either?" she asked.

"If I knew about this, how long do you think I could go without talking about it?" She seemed to accept this as an answer.

Doctor Nocturne joined us, his arms outstretched.

"What do you think? All the other entrances are still works in progress. The electrician came in and installed the emergency lights, but everything else is still on hold until the excavating is finished. You have the tunnel to your condo, Ultraviolet, over there. This wide tunnel will lead to an abandoned paint-and-body shop. And up there is the tunnel that will connect to Nate's house."

I snapped my head around.

"Does that mean my trusted advisor meets with your approval?" Ultraviolet asked with a smile.

"Assuming you still want him," Doctor Nocturne replied.

We checked out some of the computers and devices that were in the crates and looked over some blueprints for the finished room. When we started to leave, Ultraviolet rode up the elevator first.

"For tomorrow night's training, can I learn more about the crime monitor wall after the stalagmites?" I asked Doctor Nocturne.

"Tomorrow night? Tomorrow night is Christmas Eve."

"You said every night."

"I said every night until you convinced me you were ready. After last night, it's hard to deny that you are," he said. "We'll get back to training after Christmas.

And I guess you should start bringing Fiona along with you."

"Fiona? Why?"

"She's got to start learning sometime."

"Learning what?"

"How to be the Dart," he said simply. "Dart gave her his ring last night."

"I know, but just because he couldn't walk," I said. "She was just borrowing it to come help."

"No," he explained gently, "once he bestows the ring on a new bearer, the power becomes hers."

My mind reeled at this news, especially when I thought of how Fiona would react.

Doctor Nocturne ignored my shocked expression and continued. "Plus, tomorrow night, I owe Captain Zombie a game of Pictionary." He muttered the last part, sounding a bit embarrassed.

"What was that?" I asked.

"I said I owe Captain Zombie a game of Pictionary. To thank him for the help he gave us. Tommy and the Dart are joining us. From what you guys were saying, though, I don't think I want to be on Zombie's team. He sounds like a terrible guesser."

"It's not all his fault. He and Teddy don't work well together," I said.

"I'll team him up with the Dart—though I guess I should stop calling him the Dart. Have to just call him Hubert."

"For that matter, if you're not Doctor Nocturne anymore, what should I call you?"

He shrugged. "I guess we need to figure that out. What do you think of Mastermind?"

"Isn't that already taken?"

"Or maybe we want it to be something about how I help superheroes get set up, like a hero engineer. Herogineer?"

"That might be the worst name ever."

"How about something relating to chess? Checkmate?"

"Wait—why do you need a nickname? What's your real name?"

"Orpheus."

"Okay," I conceded. "Let's figure out a nickname."

Check out all the action in Nate's next adventure!

As soon as we entered the zoo, everyone around us turned to the right, ignoring the nocturnal predator exhibit to the left and the re-creation of an African savannah straight ahead. Nobody so much as slowed his pace as he passed the orangutans, gorillas, and chimpanzees in the Primates Pavilion. Thousands of people had turned out for one reason only—to see Shu Fang the panda.

"This is crazy, Dad," my sister Denise complained. "Can we go home?"

Mom agreed. "The panda is going to be here for six months. Why don't we come back some other time when it isn't so crowded?"

"We're almost there," Dad assured us, standing on his tiptoes to see over the crowd. "It's right up there. Nate, try going to the left. The crowd's a little thinner over there."

I worked my way between people who all had the same thought my dad did. Eventually I reached the railing of the rhinoceros habitat and could go no farther.

Dad shrugged. "Well, I guess now we wait."

"Shu Fang is one of fewer than three thousand pandas in existence," a recorded voice announced.

After five minutes, we'd only gotten about four inches closer to Shu Fang. Denise renewed her request to leave, but by now the crowd behind us was as thick as the crowd in front of us.

"The panda is an omnivore, though its diet consists almost entirely of bamboo," the recorded voice continued.

"An adult panda can eat as much as thirty pounds of bamboo every day."

I climbed up the rhino railing to get a better view of what lay ahead. Denise gave me a shove, and I spun around, steadying myself by gripping the rail.

"Very funny!" I yelled. "Do you want me to fall in with the rhinoceros?" It was about a fifteen-foot drop from the railing to the pit where the rhinos lived.

But Denise hadn't pushed me to be mean. The person behind her had pushed her into me, and that was because the person behind *him* had been pushed. In fact, from my higher vantage point, I could see the crowd rippling forward as bodies slammed into one another.

In my pocket, I felt the vibration of the crisis monitor I carried at all times. Turning back toward the zoo entrance, I saw a man whose head rose above the rest of the crowd. His shoulders were as wide as two men standing side by side. He wore a black suit coat, a red-striped tie, and a tiny black cap. I couldn't see his legs, but I knew he was wearing short pants.

"Schoolboy Krush," I muttered.

"Hey, quit pushing," someone nearby shouted as another wave of Schoolboy's progress rippled through the crowd. The giant of a man was moving people aside with sweeps of his massive arms, as though he was swimming through the crowd toward the panda.

I reached one hand into my pocket to pull out the crisis monitor. Its small video screen showed a map of Kanigher Falls with a red dot flashing over the zoo.

"No, really?" I grumbled.

Because I was staring at the screen, I didn't notice when the next wave of shoving came through. Denise's shoulder collided with my thigh, knocking me off balance. My left foot slipped off the railing and I toppled backward into the rhino pit. Instinctively, my arm shot out to grip the railing, letting loose my grip on the crisis monitor, which tumbled into a mud puddle below with a squishy *plop*.

"Development in China has wiped out most of the panda's natural lowland habitat," the recorded voice informed the now panicking crowd.

I gripped the bottom railing with both hands, letting my legs swing around and slam me into the rhino enclosure's sloped wall. I heard my dad shout my name, but I was focusing on the crisis monitor in the mud beneath me. Pulling myself up would have been easy, but if Ultraviolet needed my help, the monitor was only way for us to communicate.

With a deep, reluctant breath, I let go of the railing and slid down the rough, steep incline as my dad shouted my name. My feet hit the muck and each slipped in a different direction, which meant that I was soon waist deep in mud. At least, I hoped it was mud.

I grabbed the crisis monitor and wiped a thick layer of mud from its screen.

"Nate!" my mom shouted. "Sit tight! We'll get you out of there."

"Forget that," Denise yelled. "Run, you idiot!"

Early in my training, Doctor Nocturne had taught me the two most important rules of success as a superhero: be aware of your surroundings and don't do anything stupid. And I had broken them both.

I looked up from the crisis monitor's readout to find myself nose to nose with the horn of a rhinoceros. He did not look happy to see me.